Demon Hunters 1: Blood Sacrifice

Demon Hunters 1
Blood Sacrifice

Avril Sabine

Cracked Acorn Productions
Australia

Demon Hunters 1: Blood Sacrifice

Published by

Cracked Acorn Productions

PO Box 1365

Gympie, Queensland 4570

Australia

email: office@crackedacornproductions.com

978-1-925131-01-7 (Kindle)

978-1-925617-37-5 (EPUB)

978-1-925131-18-5 (Print)

Genre: Young Adult Urban Fantasy/Horror

*For Cat, who is always willing to help me
with research no matter how crazy it seems.*

Everyone knows about stranger danger. Never talk to a stranger. Don't take candy from a stranger. And no matter what, never, ever accept a ride from a stranger. In a moment of anger at her parents, eighteen-year-old Alyssa ignored these basic rules. Now she's facing the most terrifying situation of her life. A world of demons, sacrifices and swords suddenly becomes her reality. Not many people survive demon encounters and Alyssa fears she might not either.

*

This story was written by an Australian author using Australian spelling.

Chapter One

Alyssa's eyes narrowed, anger making it impossible to speak.

Grace, her mother, stood with a hand on her hip, her foot tapping. "Well?"

The words exploded from Alyssa. "I'm eighteen. I've finished year twelve and start uni next year. I'm not a kid. Stop treating me like one."

"Do not raise your voice to me."

"You're not listening."

"When you stop acting like a child, I will."

"A party. A stupid bloody party. What do you think I'm going to do there?" Alyssa's hands tightened into fists. She wanted to throw something. She'd thought turning eighteen last week would change things. Most of her friends had been given more freedom when they turned fifteen.

"I've already said no. That's enough. I don't want to hear another word."

"Why? Why can't I go?"

"You can't. Stop questioning me. As long as you live under our roof, you live by our rules."

Alyssa glared at Grace. She hated the way everyone said she looked like her mother. So she wore her dark hair layered, to fall past her shoulders, and had a purple streak in it that curved from the crown of her head to frame her left cheek. There was nothing she could do about their matching green eyes, high cheekbones and honey coloured skin.

Grace turned away, stepping around the wooden table and chairs in the middle of the kitchen.

"Then maybe it's time I left home," Alyssa said.

Grace spun to face her. "And how do you think you'll live? Food doesn't appear on the table because you're hungry." Her mother's hand returned to her hip. "Well? You haven't got an answer for that, have you?"

Anger burned through Alyssa, hotter than before. Her teeth clamped together. "I hear you can make a good living on the streets. Maybe I should find out for myself." She grinned bitterly, satisfied at the expression on her mother's face. Before her mother could recover, Alyssa spun on her heel and strode for the front door, flinging the words over her shoulder, "Guess I'll be back if I can't find any customers." As she reached the door, she heard her mother's hurried footsteps behind her.

"Don't you dare walk out that door."

"Or what? I can't walk back in? Yeah. Real loss." Alyssa shoved the screen door open as she grabbed her handbag from the hallstand. She pulled the strap over her head and tugged on it so the bag slid across her hip to a more comfortable position.

"I'm serious."

Alyssa looked over her shoulder, her gaze clashing with her mother's. She hesitated, mentally cataloguing what was in her handbag. Money, make-up, change of clothes for the party, her phone and various unknown items that had been thrown in there and forgotten about in the year she'd owned it.

"Alyssa."

The warning tone in Grace's voice was all Alyssa needed to make up her mind. She knew if she gave in, she'd spend her four years at university living by her parents' rules. A simple party! It wasn't even like she was asking to go to Schoolies. She wasn't a child. She was sick of being treated like one. Another rush of anger hit her at the injustice.

This time she managed to keep her voice low. "So

am I." She stepped through the doorway, letting the screen door bang shut. She grabbed her knee-high black boots off the verandah, paused at the top of the stairs to lean against the post to pull them on and zipped them up.

"Alyssa! I'm ringing your father!"

Alyssa laughed harshly. "Go ahead. What's he going to do? Drag me home again? Tell him to go ahead and try. But he's got to find me first." Alyssa took every second step in her haste. Before she'd reached the concrete footpath, her phone was at her ear so she could call her best friend to say she was going to the party.

Alyssa held the phone away from her ear at Erin's shout. "Great, now I'm deaf."

"I can't believe they're letting you go. I thought they'd keep you under lock and key until you were thirty."

"Yeah, well they tried to. But Dad's over at his mate's place. I hit Mum with it after he'd gone. I bet she's ringing him right now. Look, I'm going to catch a bus into the city. We can meet up at Del's and head to the party from there."

"What time?"

Alyssa glanced at her watch. "Probably take me a

couple of hours to get there at the most. Meet up about seven-thirty?"

"Sounds good. I'll see you there."

Alyssa hung up and slipped her phone into one of the outer pockets of her handbag, unable to resist a grin as she strode towards the bus stop. There was no way her father could be home in time to catch up with her. The bus would arrive within a couple of minutes. And even if it was late, there was another bus due in five minutes in the opposite direction. Either one, it didn't matter. As long as she put some distance between her and home she could take the scenic route into the city.

* * *

Alyssa sat on one of the cold metal chairs in the noisy interior of Del's. The table was equally as solid as the chairs, since Del's couldn't go a week without at least one fight breaking out. But Del, a large man who looked more like he belonged in a boxing ring than behind the counter in a coffee shop, would slowly make his way to the offending parties, grab each by the collar and drag them outside. No threats, no warnings. He'd shut the door and head to his counter as if nothing had happened.

Alyssa took a bite of her burger and glanced around. She knew probably half the crowd. Some well, some by sight, many from the high school she'd recently graduated from. The sound of the door opening again had her glancing over and she quickly swallowed her mouthful.

Waving, Alyssa called out, "Erin."

Erin grinned and made her way through the crowded tables. She slid into the seat across from Alyssa and dropped her bag on the floor. Erin was a few inches shorter than Alyssa and people called her dainty or cute and the occasional unfortunate called her a doll since her resemblance to a blue eyed, blond haired, porcelain doll was uncanny. The words always made Erin see red and having four older brothers had taught her how to hold her own in a fight.

"Where's mine?" Erin glanced towards the burger.

"Split it?" Alyssa offered.

Erin frowned. "Guess that'll have to do. I haven't the time to wait for one. I don't want to miss even a minute of this party."

"What about late enough to make an entrance?"

"Who cares about making an entrance? I'd rather have all the fun." Erin took the half a burger Alyssa held out. "No one makes a burger like Del." She took a large bite and her eyes closed theatrically.

Alyssa laughed. "It's just a burger, Erin. No need to make out with it."

"Blasphemy. This is not just a burger."

"Hey."

Alyssa glanced up at the young man who had stopped at their table. He had the same fine blond hair and blue eyes as Erin, but his narrow frame was taller. "Aiden."

"So who let you out of jail?" Aiden, the brother closest to Erin in age, mocked.

"Get lost, Aiden," Erin muttered. "Can't you be like any normal older brother and act like you don't know me?"

"Nope. No fun in that now, is there?"

Erin sighed heavily, then her blue eyes widened. "No!"

"No, what?" Aiden's grin broadened.

"You're not going to Kylie's party are you?"

"Who else is going to make sure the guys behave themselves around you?"

Erin groaned. "I swear I'll kill you if you have a 'word' with any guy I talk to at the party. I don't need you to look out for me. I can take care of myself."

"Would I do that?" Aiden tried for an innocent expression.

"You're dead. You got that? Dead."

Aiden chuckled. "See you there, brat."

"Aiden!" Erin leapt to her feet, burger clutched in one hand. Her only answer was a wave from Aiden who didn't even bother to turn at her call.

"Just great!" Erin slumped into her seat. "The party's ruined. Why do my brothers have to do this? I can take care of myself."

"At least you're allowed to go to parties. Your brothers are a small price to pay. Come on. Eat your burger so we can go," Alyssa encouraged.

"Easy for you to say. You're so lucky being an only child."

"Maybe my parents wouldn't be overkill if they had more kids."

They shared a look and then grinned at the same time and shook their heads. "Nah," Erin said as Alyssa said, "Not."

Alyssa finished off the last of her burger and licked her fingers clean. "I'm going to the bathroom to change and do my make-up. Be back in a few."

Erin nodded, her mouth full.

The chair scraped across the floor as Alyssa stood and wove her way through the crowd. She pushed the bathroom door open and there was an instant quiet as it swung shut. A girl stood at the mirror filling the wall behind the hand basins, fixing her hair.

Alyssa made her way to the far end of the bathroom, did her makeup then brushed her hair, running it through the purple streak last.

The bathroom door flew open. Erin stood in the doorway. "What's taking so long?"

"Nearly finished." Alyssa headed into one of the toilet cubicles and locked the door. She hung her bag on the hook near the top of the door and started to change her clothes, replacing her jeans with a short skirt.

"All the fun'll be over if you don't hurry."

"Erin!" Alyssa's voice was sharp as she tugged her skirt into place.

"Okay. Fine. I'm shutting up."

Alyssa grinned as she changed her shirt. Her friend was permanently impatient. And she'd be surprised if Erin lasted thirty seconds without trying to hurry her. She glanced at her watch then decided to use the timer on her phone. It was still off. She'd forgotten she'd turned it off when her parents wouldn't stop ringing earlier. There was no point using it to time Erin, but maybe she could turn it back on now. Surely they'd have got the message and given up ringing.

"Allie?"

Alyssa chuckled. She turned her phone on and

shoved her roughly folded jeans and shirt into her bag. Grinning, she swung the door open and held up her phone. "I was going to time how long it took before you started again. But I knew the phone would take too long to turn on."

"Very funny," Erin said dryly. "Can we go now?"

"Sure." Alyssa glanced at the girl still standing by the mirror. The girl threw a nervous glance towards Erin.

As soon as they were outside Del's, Alyssa asked Erin, "What did you do to her?"

"Who?"

"The girl in the bathroom." Alyssa had to lengthen her stride to keep up with Erin who believed life should be taken at a run.

"Nothing."

"Sure," Alyssa said dryly. "I recognise that tone."

"She was staring at me. I hate it when people stare at me." Erin glared at her.

Alyssa laughed. "You know that look won't work with me. I've known you too long. But that poor kid in the bathroom, I'm surprised she didn't run out screaming. Actually, on second thought, I know why she didn't. You were blocking the only exit."

Before Erin could comment, Alyssa's phone started

to ring. She checked to see who the caller was and frowned when she saw it was her home number.

Erin tilted Alyssa's hand to peer at the screen. "They must be calling every ten minutes or something." She let go of Alyssa's hand. "Or they've got really good timing."

Alyssa shoved the ringing phone in her bag. "I wish I could afford to move out. But working part-time at the bakery doesn't give me enough money to pay for rent let alone food and everything else."

"At least you don't have to share a bathroom with four brothers."

"No, but I get to constantly argue with my parents even though I always tell myself I'm not going to. They treat me like a kid who has no clue and then I start acting like one. They push all the wrong buttons."

"Parents are good at that."

"Well mine certainly are." Alyssa gritted her teeth as her phone started to ring again.

"Oh please, answer it," Erin groaned. "It was bad enough having to listen to it ring out once. I'll be tempted to throw it in front of the next car that passes if you don't."

Alyssa answered her phone. "What?"

"Tell me where you are and I'll send your father to

pick you up and we'll forget all about this incident," Grace said.

"No."

"Alyssa–"

"Quit ringing me. I'm going to the party and that's final."

A car horn made Erin and Alyssa turn towards the road. Three young men in a sleek, black car pulled over.

"Want a ride, ladies?" The one in the back seat leaned out the window.

"What is happening?" Grace demanded.

"We're busy hitchhiking and someone just pulled over to give us a lift." Alyssa's words dripped with sarcasm.

"Don't you dare," Grace warned.

"Allie," Erin said hesitantly from beside her.

"Where are you going?" The man called out. "You look like you've got a destination in mind. How about we all go?"

"Alyssa!" Grace screeched in her ear. "Daniel, come and talk some sense into your daughter."

Alyssa guessed her mother had covered the phone with her hand to tell her father what was going on. But even that couldn't mute his bellow.

"We haven't got all night. It might only be young

now, but the night's rapidly ageing." The man let the car door swing open. "Plenty of space."

"Allie, please." Erin stepped away, her clasped hands pressed tightly to her chest.

Alyssa took a step towards Erin, starting to take the phone from her ear. She halted at her father's angry tone.

"Alyssa Ann Evans! You will tell me where you are immediately. You will not hitchhike. You aren't too old I can't ground you. This is beyond belief. You keep trying to tell us you're an adult, well act like one."

Blind rage coursed through Alyssa. "Get stuffed," she snarled at her father and turned her phone off before she dropped it in her bag. She stepped forward, eyes sparking with anger, a forced smile on her lips.

"Well, hey," the man scooted over. "Hop right on in."

Alyssa rested one hand on the car roof, the other on the top of the door and leaned forward a little. All three men looked to be in their early twenties. Two had close cropped, dark hair while the one in the back wore his a little longer.

"I'm only going a couple of blocks that way to a party." Alyssa waved in the direction they had been heading. "I'm Allie."

"Nathan. That's Eric," he pointed to the driver, "And Shawn."

"Allie!" Erin stayed well back from the vehicle. "We're going to be late."

Alyssa hesitated, glancing at her friend. When Nathan spoke she turned towards him.

"No you won't. We'll have you there in no time, won't we guys?" Nathan appealed to his companions who instantly agreed. He smiled up at her. "Hop on in, Allie."

Her hesitation evaporated at his smile. Reassurance filled her. "Thanks." Alyssa slid into the car to sit beside him. "These boots aren't exactly made for walking long distances. And I've already walked too far in them today."

"What about your friend? She coming too?"

"Erin?" Alyssa watched as her friend shook her head, taking another step back.

"You're mad. I'm walking. No, better yet, I'm calling Aiden." Erin pulled her phone out.

"See you shortly." Alyssa reached out and pulled the car door shut, buckling up. She smiled at Nathan with a shrug. "I guess not."

"All right then. We'll see her at the party. A pity since she was so worried about being late."

Eric pulled away from the curb. "So where's this party?"

Alyssa leaned forward to explain the directions. She felt a quick sharp pain in her arm and looked down. Her mouth opened silently as she saw the needle being withdrawn. She stared at Nathan.

"Guess you should have listened to your friend, huh?" Nathan pushed her back into the seat, another smile curving his lips. "I think tonight's going to be a bit different than you expected."

Alyssa couldn't think clearly and it felt like the world was fading. The reassurance she had felt last time he smiled didn't come. This time it was fear. A cold fear that skittered through her body and froze limbs and vocal cords. The last thing she saw was Nathan's deep brown eyes watching her slip away. She was surprised to see they were filled with mocking amusement.

Chapter Two

Alyssa slowly came to. A pounding in her head and a horrible taste in her mouth let her know she was alive. She tried to move her arms. Panic rushed through her when she couldn't. They were tied above her head. The rest of her body could move and she twisted, realising she was on a narrow, metal-framed bed.

A scream threatened to escape and Alyssa held it in. As she twisted to see more of where she was being held, her foot brushed against something at the end of the bed. A sudden indrawn breath, fists clenched and teeth clamped together was enough to hold in the scream a little longer. She lifted her head and saw it was her handbag. She let out the breath she held.

The room was nearly empty. Grey light shone feebly in from an uncurtained window. The light of predawn did little to dispel the darkness in the small, featureless room. Other than the bed, there was only a solid looking armchair. The room was also devoid of other people.

Alyssa strained her ears, but could hear nothing. She was alone. As hard as she tried to convince herself being alone was preferable to being with one of the men who'd kidnapped her, the thought of being tied up and unable to escape seemed far worse. No one knew where she was. She didn't even know where she was. The thought of being tied up for days until she starved raced through her mind. Her stomach growled as if to highlight her predicament.

Alyssa fought a wild urge to laugh. Hysteria, she thought. And I can't even slap myself out of it. More laughter threatened. A quick indrawn breath turned into a half sob. "Think," she whispered to herself. Her foot brushed against her bag again. The image of her phone flashed into her mind. Carefully, so she didn't knock it off the bed, Alyssa tugged at the bag with her feet. She moved up on the bed, until she sat with her back against the bed head and her arms held awkwardly to one side. She hooked her foot around her bag and pulled it ever closer. She had her boots on and they made the procedure difficult. As did her skirt.

A sudden scrape at the door made her freeze, her gaze darting towards it. She began to tremble. Her breath shuddered in and out as she tried to control the urge to scream. She was worried if she started she'd never stop.

The door swung open and Nathan stood in the doorway, a tray of food balanced on one hand. "And sleeping beauty wakes right on schedule."

"Why?" The word came out as little more than a croak.

"If you be a good girl I'll untie one hand and let you have something to eat."

"I want to go home." Alyssa could only manage a whisper.

"I hope you're not going to cry. Tears annoy the hell out of me." He placed the tray on the floor beside the bed and straightened to stare down at her.

Alyssa looked into the same dark eyes that had been her last vision before this room. The faint hint of amusement was back in them. Anger started to course through her, chasing away the fear.

Nathan laughed. "And don't you look like you could go several rounds in the ring right now. It's not going to help you know."

"I need to use the bathroom," Alyssa said coldly, a sharpness to her tone. Anger she knew. It was almost a friend.

His eyes narrowed. Then, with a single nod, he

untied Alyssa from the bed frame. He held her wrists tightly and stared into her eyes, all amusement currently gone from his. "You try and escape and next time you need to go to the bathroom I won't be taking you."

Alyssa didn't answer, only returned his stare. Behind her anger was the fear she'd felt on waking. The mind numbing fear that had gripped her before the drug had done its job last night. And she didn't want to let it take over again. She fought to hold onto her anger, but a persistent thought kept trying to force its way past it. Nathan hadn't bothered to hide his face. She could describe him in perfect detail to the police if she was ever released. She could think of only one reason he hadn't bothered to hide his face. And that reason involved her not being able to tell anyone.

Nathan let go of her wrists and stepped back. "You've got fifteen minutes. Turn right, second door on the left." He motioned towards the door he'd left open.

Alyssa glanced towards him and then the doorway. She automatically grabbed her handbag and started to slide off the bed.

"The bag stays here."

Alyssa's fingers tightened on the strap before she

forced them to let go. She concentrated on standing up from the bed and watched as her boots touched the wooden floorboards. She continued to stare at them as she took a hesitant step forward. It was easier to watch where her feet landed than to give any attention to the man who stood to her left. Easier to focus on putting one foot in front of the other than to let unsettling thoughts enter her head. One foot in front of the other. She paused in the doorway, her gaze drawn to the left. There was a closed door several metres from her. She looked towards the right and saw the corridor ended in a T intersection.

"Time's ticking, Princess."

Nathan was so close she could feel his breath graze her cheek. Her head flew up and she stumbled into the corridor as she spun to face him. His grin made the anger in her burn brighter. She turned away from him and forced herself to walk at a normal pace to the bathroom. What she really wanted to do was run. Run as far and as fast as possible. And scream. She wanted to scream until she was so hoarse she could scream no more. And even then, she thought she might continue. Only silently. Mouth open. Sound absent.

Seeing the second door on the left, Alyssa stopped in front of it. She focused all her attention on the door. Anything to prevent herself from sending a fearful glance to Nathan. Was he standing in the doorway? Had he followed her silently again? She reached out and turned the doorknob. The door opened easily and she stepped inside the bathroom. She leaned against the door once she closed it and saw it had a lock. The sound of it clicking into place was satisfying.

Still leaned against the door, Alyssa glanced around. White tiles, pale blue trim. It was only large enough for a shower, toilet and a vanity with a large mirror on the wall behind it. Even the window was small, three short louvres set high up on the wall above the toilet. Alyssa started to slide down the door, her knees wanting to give way.

But she didn't know how much time she had left. She forced her rubbery legs to carry her to the toilet and once she'd used it, leaned against the vanity, staring at herself in the mirror. Her eyes looked too large for her face, haunted green pools. Too large and too full of emotions she didn't want to admit to. She splashed water on her face and tried to clean off the smeared makeup. A hand towel hung on the wall beside her and she used it to wipe most of it off. She left the discoloured cloth on the vanity, not caring if it was ruined. She hoped it was. Grim satisfaction momentarily arrowed through her. She cupped her hands under the tap and drank, the water doing little to ease the hunger pains. While the water ran over her hands, she realised her watch was missing. What else had been taken from her while she slept? She couldn't focus on that thought so she looked up, away from her bare wrist. In the mirror, she could see the small window.

She had to get out. Panic rushed at her, stealing her breath and making her cling to the vanity as her legs gave out. She slid to the floor. Her hands clung to the edge of the vanity and her head pressed against the doors. A shuddering sob tore through her.

"Time's up. Get out here now," Nathan ordered from the other side of the door.

Alyssa started to shake, and her teeth chattered as if she was cold. The water continued to run in the basin and Nathan banged on the door. Alyssa couldn't move or talk. It was all she could do not to scream.

"If I have to break down this door, you won't like the consequences." Nathan spoke softly, but Alyssa had no trouble believing he meant every word.

She crawled across the floor, unable to stand and with a trembling hand reached up and unlocked the door. She moved to the side as the door swung open. She kept her head down so her hair fell forward to hide her face. Her eyes closed so she didn't have to see her surroundings. She wished she was somewhere else. Anywhere else. Her body continued to shake and if her teeth hadn't been clenched so tightly, they'd have chattered.

The silence stretched out and she was tempted to open her eyes and see if Nathan still stood there. But she'd rather keep them closed and imagine he'd left. Keep them closed and think about the party she was supposed to go to. She thought of Erin, probably frantic by now. Would she have called her parents? Would people be looking for her?

Her thoughts were brought to an abrupt end as he grabbed her arm and dragged her roughly to her feet. Her head snapped back and her eyes flew open. She stared up at Nathan.

How could I have got into a car with him? So he's good looking. Big deal. Don't they say some of the worst serial killers are?

"You'll ring the girl you were with. And tell her you're fine." Nathan pressed her phone into her hands.

"No."

"We can track her down. Do you want us to do that? It'd be best if she had no reason to describe us to the police."

Alyssa's fingers closed around her phone. "It's probably too late."

"You'd better hope it isn't. Now ring her. And make sure you don't say the wrong thing. Be convincing. I don't leave loose threads behind."

Alyssa trembled at the lack of emotion in Nathan's voice. She couldn't look away from his eyes. Even the amusement from earlier was gone. Now they were as emotionless as his voice.

"Why?" The word came out like a plea and Alyssa cringed to hear herself.

"Ring your friend now."

Chapter Three

Nathan let go of Alyssa and she stumbled, catching herself on the wall. She knew her legs wouldn't hold her for more than a few seconds, they trembled that hard. She slid down the wall until she sat at Nathan's feet. It was the last place she wanted to be, but she had little choice in the matter. When Nathan looked pointedly at her phone again, she turned it on. She cringed back against the wall as Nathan moved towards her. She shuddered in relief when she saw he was only turning the tap off.

When her phone finished turning on, she stared at the date and time displayed over a photo of her and Erin. Nearly six a.m. Yesterday her life had been normal. Yesterday her biggest problem had been her parents.

"What are you waiting for?"

Alyssa glanced towards Nathan before she called

Erin. Her friend answered instantly, which was amazing at this hour of the morning.

"Where are you? I've been frantic. I even called the police, but they said you hadn't been missing for twenty-four hours and you went with them of your own free will and-" Erin fell silent for about five seconds. "Oh god, no. It is you, isn't it? Speak to me."

"It's me." Alyssa tried hard to make her voice sound normal. "It's just impossible to talk over you." She closed her eyes and blocked out her surroundings, concentrating on Erin. She had to keep Erin safe.

"Where are you?"

"Nathan's house."

"You've got to be kidding me. What the hell do you think you're doing? Are you mad?"

"Probably."

"What's the address? I'll get one of my brothers to pick you up."

"Erin. I'm fine. I'm going to hang out with Nathan today."

"But you don't even know him. For all you know he could be a serial killer."

Alyssa started to laugh. She tried hard to stop, but it seemed impossible. Tears streamed down her cheeks and she tried to convince herself it was from laughter.

"Allie? You okay? You sound.... I don't know. You're not in some kind of trouble are you?"

"Sorry. But it was just... so funny." Alyssa forced herself to stop laughing by reminding herself Erin needed to be kept safe. "Did you say anything to my parents about... last night?"

"Nearly. But, well... I didn't want to get you into more trouble. I didn't know what to do. I mean you just hopped in the car. And then you weren't at the party. You should have called me."

"I'm sorry."

"Yeah well, don't you ever do that to me again."

"Look, I've got to go. I'll give you a call later."

"Make sure you do. I've been so worried about you. Call me every hour so I know you're alive."

"Really, Erin. That's overkill. It's something my parents'd say. I'll call you later when I get a few minutes. We've got things we're planning to do."

"Like what?"

"I'll tell you everything when I see you next."

"Promise?"

"Yeah, Erin. I promise. After all, you're my best friend. And isn't that what best friends do?"

"Aww, don't go getting mushy on me."

"Talk to you later."

"Okay."

Alyssa hung up and let her hand drop into her lap. Her eyes stayed closed and she didn't have a clue if Nathan stood there watching her. Her cheeks were damp with tears and her throat ached with trying to hold the rest of them back. Something nudged her leg and her eyes flew open. It was Nathan's boot. Her gaze travelled up the black denim that covered his legs and stopped at the dark green shirt he wore. She couldn't bring herself to look at his face. To look into his eyes. If they were filled with amusement she knew she'd be tempted to strike him. Well, she would if she could figure out how to make her body move.

"Back to the room now. Before I drag you."

"Drag me then," Alyssa muttered.

"Then don't bother asking to use the bathroom again," Nathan warned.

"Bastard!" She tried to struggle to her feet. She closed her eyes tight for a second before she opened them again. This time she met Nathan's gaze, her hand held out towards him. "Help me up." It took an effort. Nearly a minute before she could bring herself to mutter, "Please."

He made her wait long enough she began to think he wouldn't bother. She was about to put her hand down when he grabbed it and dragged her to her feet. She swayed as she held tightly to his hand. It was a lifeline. A reluctant one. But she was even more reluctant to fall flat on her face. As soon as she was steady, she let go of his hand and walked back to her prison. Her phone was clutched tightly, her knuckles white from the pressure.

Alyssa paused in the doorway, her gaze drawn to the bed. She looked at the armchair. That was her only option. She couldn't bring herself to go anywhere near the bed. As soon as she reached the chair, she collapsed into it.

"Back on the bed. I can't chain you to the chair." Nathan stood in the doorway.

"I-" Alyssa stopped speaking the moment she looked into his eyes. Pleading would be a waste of breath.

"And your phone. Hand it over. You can keep the rest of your junk."

Alyssa glanced to where she'd left her handbag on the bed and noticed the contents had been dumped out. Anger surged through her and brought her to her feet. "How dare you-" she broke off at his laughter.

"You're more amusing than the last one."

"Last-" Alyssa seemed to be having trouble finishing sentences. She took several steps towards the bed. She wanted to gather all her things and hold them tight. It was irrational. She knew it was. They were things. Unimportant. Having her bag searched was nothing compared to being drugged and kidnapped.

"Your phone, Allie."

Alyssa looked at it. Her only contact with the rest of the world. She took several reluctant steps towards Nathan. As she started to hand the phone to him, it began to ring. She nearly dropped it. She glanced at the display before she looked at Nathan. "My parents."

"Answer them. And don't forget I know where they live. I saw the address on your license."

Alyssa nodded and answered her phone.

"I've been out of my mind with worry all night. We won't tolerate this sort of behaviour."

"Sorry, Mum. But you're suffocating me."

"Don't be ridiculous. You're our child. Of course we're going to protect you. Where are you?"

"With a friend. Look, I'm going to stay here for a bit. As much as I love you and Dad, I really need a break from you."

"Stop acting so childish and tell me where you are," Grace snapped. "Do I have to wake your father to talk to you?"

"I'm sorry for everything. I love you, Mum. I'm

turning my phone off now and leaving it off. I'm really sorry." Her words broke on a reluctant sob. Alyssa turned her phone off before she could cry and handed it to Nathan who pushed it into the back pocket of his jeans.

"On the bed."

Alyssa turned towards the bed and froze. She couldn't do it. She couldn't make herself walk to the bed. She knew he was going to tie her up, but then what? And what last one? How many had there been before her and what had happened to them? A push against her lower back caused her to stumble forward, and she had to step sideways so she didn't land in the tray of food beside the bed. She lost her balance and tumbled onto the bed, trying to avoid falling on her things. She twisted as she fell so she lay on her back, staring up at Nathan as he stood above her.

"I have a little present for you." With a sneer, Nathan pulled a pair of handcuffs from his back pocket and roughly grabbed one of her hands. He had her attached to the bed head in moments. "Don't go away now. We've got some fun planned for this evening."

"What sort of fun?" Alyssa was certain she didn't want to know, but the question seemed to escape on its own.

"If you're a good little girl I might tell you when I come back."

"You're going?" Hysteria threatened to erupt again.

"No one can hear you if you scream." Nathan's lips curved into a malicious smile. "I'll be back before dark. Midnight at the latest." Then he was gone and the door was locked behind him.

Alyssa focused on the fact she should've rechecked the time before handing over her phone. Time. Time seemed to be in short supply. Midnight. Was that it? Was that all the time she had left? How many minutes had she used talking on the phone? How many minutes were left? Once again she fought the scream that tried to escape. He expected her to scream. She wouldn't give him the satisfaction. There had to be some way out of this. Never had she imagined her life would end like this. Sure, she'd read books, seen movies, even read articles in newspapers and watched the news. But things like this didn't happen to people like her. Other people maybe. Not her. Maybe it was a nightmare. Alyssa latched onto that idea. Of course. A nightmare. She sat up, and looked around.

The room was in clear focus. Everything was sharp, unlike her usually blurred dreams. "Won't think about it," Alyssa muttered. Her gaze fell on the tray and she reached towards it. Her hand curled into a fist and she quickly withdrew it. Was it drugged? How could you tell? Her stomach growled. Her fist opened and her hand pressed against her mouth. Saliva filled it at the thought of the food sitting there, taunting her. She forced her gaze away from the tray. They fell on the scattered contents of her bag. In amongst everything, she spotted a chocolate bar and pounced on it. She quickly tore off the wrapper and took a large bite. It was gone within seconds and she was searching through the rest of her things. She found a small packet of chips and a nearly empty bottle of water. She drank the last mouthful of tepid water before starting on the chips.

Her stomach still felt hollow. She put everything back in her bag, one item at a time, hoping she'd missed spotting some food. All she managed to find was a brightly wrapped butterscotch. She popped the sweet in her mouth and tried not to think of the food on the floor. She could manage. Hadn't she held in the scream that echoed in the back of her head? Not touching food should be simple.

But it wasn't. It called to her. Mocked her. Determined, she stood up and pushed the tray away from the bed with the toe of her boot. She sat on the floor and lay down. She stretched out as far as possible, her arm high over her head and the handcuffs cutting into her wrist. She pushed the tray across the room with her foot. Now it'd be impossible to reach. She crawled on the bed. She couldn't give in and eat it. Satisfied, she stared sightlessly at the ceiling. In a minute she'd have a look at the handcuff. There had to be some way of getting out of it. How many movies had she seen where they'd picked the lock and escaped? How hard could it be?

A wave of despair washed over her and she closed her eyes. She fought back the tears that threatened to fall. Instead she focused on her breathing. Breathe in, breathe out. Breathe in. Breathe out. She focused so hard on her breathing she fell asleep.

Chapter Four

Alyssa turned her head into the caress that trailed across her cheek, her jaw and then along her throat. She went to reach out with her left hand, but couldn't move it. The metal of the handcuffs dug into her wrist.

Handcuffs! Alyssa's eyes flew open. Everything rushed back. She looked up at Nathan who sat beside her on the bed and saw amusement again filled his eyes. She tried to move away from him and he tightened his fingers around her throat. She froze. A bare light bulb in the ceiling above him shone in her eyes, but she couldn't look away.

His lips twisted into a sardonic smile. "I expected you to be screaming the place down by now. Instead I find you fast asleep. Odd." He stroked the pulse at her throat. "But you are scared. So why aren't you screaming?"

Alyssa knew if she started to scream she'd be swamped by blind panic. It didn't help that every time he smiled more fear rushed through her. She needed to stay as rational as possible. There had to be a way out of this nightmare. But she couldn't say that. No way was she going to warn him. "Would it help?" The words were a whisper, but at least she managed them without letting free the scream that echoed inside her head.

"So… no little rabbit to run frantically back and forth in front of the headlights. What are you then? No lion either to strike out no matter how futile. What do you think you are?"

Alyssa surprised herself by saying, "How about an ostrich? Head buried in the sand."

Nathan threw back his head and laughed. He still smiled as he met her gaze. "It'll be a pity to use you. If I could get a replacement this close I would. I think you'd be worth keeping for a bit. There's so little in life that's amusing anymore."

"Aren't you too young to think that?"

"Now that's where you're wrong. I'm nearly thirty, little ostrich."

Alyssa wished he'd move his hand from her throat. He no longer pressed against it, but she knew how easy it'd be for him to tighten his grip. "Why me?"

He lifted the lock of purple hair and twined it around his finger, the other hand stayed against her throat. "Many reasons. But basically because you looked like you might hop in. And there weren't many witnesses around."

Alyssa forced herself to ask the question she was in two minds of having answered. "What are you going to do with me?"

"I've been waiting for that question. How about I make a deal with you? Call your friend and convince her you're going somewhere without me. Doesn't matter where. You just need to remove me from the equation. Then I'll answer all your questions and I won't hunt down your friend or parents."

Alyssa knew he wasn't giving her much choice. She'd ring Erin without the incentive of her questions answered. "I need to use the bathroom first." After his earlier threats she wanted to make sure he wouldn't leave her handcuffed to the bed until she wet herself. Even though she knew it was a minor concern, at least it was a concern she could deal with. One step at a time.

Nathan continued to look down at her, his eyes emotionless again. Then he moved off the bed. He took a key from his shirt pocket and unlocked the handcuff from the bed. He let it dangle from her wrist. "Make it quick."

This time when Alyssa slung her handbag over her shoulder, Nathan didn't stop her. He stood to the side as she stumbled to the door. When Alyssa glanced at the tray of food, he laughed and she looked over at him.

"It would have made it a lot easier on you if you'd eaten it."

Alyssa took that as confirmation the food was drugged and the hollow pit in her stomach seemed justified. She hurried to the bathroom, worried Nathan might change his mind. The moment she was in there, she locked the door. As soon as she'd used the toilet, she rinsed and filled the bottle she'd found in her bag earlier. She drank from the tap and then turned it off. The handcuffs hit the metal and she cringed at the sound.

A movement caught her attention and she looked up to stare at her reflection. It felt like she looked at someone else. Even her mind barely registered any thought. Alyssa was glad of the numbness that seemed to settle in. The scream echoed in there, but not many other thoughts surfaced. Or those that did, she brutally shoved away. She couldn't think. Not without becoming a rabbit. She had to stay calm and in control. Well, as much in control as a person held against their will could be. She looked at the window again. If only it was larger. Pushing that thought from her mind, she forced herself to unlock the door.

Nathan leaned against the wall across from the bathroom. He said nothing. He watched her as she paused in the doorway. She stood there and waited to see what he'd do. He pushed away from the wall and handed her phone to her before he walked back to her prison. She looked down at it then over to Nathan as he stepped into the room. Was she meant to follow? She took a few steps forward. Maybe he was going to let her call her friend without listening in. She didn't know. It seemed unlikely. So she walked to her prison and stopped in the doorway.

Nathan sat in the armchair. That only left the bed. If she didn't need to sit so badly she wouldn't have considered it. But her legs felt wobbly and she knew if she didn't sit soon they'd give out on her.

Alyssa dialled Erin's number. She picked up on the second ring.

"What have you been doing all day? I've been waiting and waiting for you to call. It's nearly seven p.m. Over twelve hours I've waited. You should've called before now."

"Sorry, Erin. I guess I was having so much fun I

lost track of time." Alyssa glared at Nathan as she said this, and was annoyed to see her words amused him. She could barely believe she'd slept the entire day. Maybe it was from the drugs she'd been given the night before. Another question she couldn't answer.

"So where are you? What have you been doing? When are you coming home?" Erin fired the questions at Alyssa, without pause for breath.

"Slow down." Alyssa forced herself to laugh. It was her usual response to her friend's inability to go slow.

"You know you could've invited me along if the day's been that much fun."

Alyssa closed her eyes. A wave of relief rushed through her that Erin had been sensible enough not to hop in the car with her last night. Last night! It seemed like it was so much longer than that.

"Allie? You still there?"

"Yeah. Sorry. I was distracted. Hey listen. We went to the beach and I ran into some people that are heading to Cairns. They've got a job at a resort up there and one of the girls going with them pulled out at the last minute so I said I'd take her place."

"You what? Are you totally insane? What about Nathan?"

"Oh, I left him at the beach with his mates and their

girlfriends. This was too good to pass up. I've always wanted to see far north Queensland."

"Allie? You sure everything's okay? You're not in any sort of trouble are you?"

Alyssa forced herself to laugh again. "Do you think I'd be ringing you to chat if I was? Really Erin, you've been watching too many horror movies."

"And you haven't been watching enough. You can't just take off with people you've met for only a few seconds."

"I can't go home either."

"Have you told your parents?"

"No. I'm just going to text them. It'll be easier."

"Ring me every day to let me know you're safe."

"I can't. My phone's running low on credit. I'll text you."

"How will I know it's you?"

"Erin! Who else is likely to send you daily text messages from my phone? Get real."

Erin laughed. "I guess. But this is so unlike you. I nearly died when you hopped in that car. I thought I'd never see you again. Don't keep doing stupid things like that. Please?"

"I swear I'll live as safely as an eighty-year-old woman once I get to Cairns."

"Great. I'm going to hold you to that."

Before Erin could continue, Alyssa changed the topic. "Did Aiden turn up at the party last night?"

"Of course."

Alyssa smiled as she let Erin complain about her brother for a bit. She eventually interrupted. "I need to go or I won't even have enough credit to text you. Bye Erin." There was so much more she wanted to say. So many things she couldn't voice without alerting Erin to the fact she was in trouble. The worst trouble she'd ever been in her entire life.

"Okay. Later."

Alyssa hung up and stared at her phone. She needed to send a text message to her parents. How was she going to word it? She continued to stare blankly at it. No words came to her mind. Pain shot through her as she thought of how her relationship with her parents had deteriorated in the past seven years. Would they blame themselves for her death? How could she make them understand this was her own stupidity?

"You going to send that message? Time's wasting, Princess."

She wished there was something she could throw at him. Anything. She wanted to wipe that look of amusement from his face. But there was nothing. The room was almost empty. And she wasn't throwing any of her things. They were hers. All that was left of her old life. All that was left of her life because it didn't look like there was going to be a way out of this situation. Alyssa stopped that thought the moment it arrived.

I'll find a way, she thought fiercely. She opened her contact list to text her parents when it started to ring. It was her home number. She had to admire her mother's persistence. And yet in her they called it stubbornness and complained.

"Who is it?" Nathan demanded.

"My parents."

"Answer it."

"No."

Nathan rose to his feet, and strode towards the bed. Alyssa looked up at him. A shiver of fear darted through her body as he towered over her. She banished the feeling and tried to regain the numbness of earlier.

"Answer the phone, now." Each word was spoken softly as his eyes bore into her.

"I can't. They'll hear the lies in my words."

The phone stopped ringing, but Nathan continued to tower over her. She couldn't look away from him. The image of a rabbit caught in headlights came to her mind and she pushed it away. She was no rabbit.

But still she continued to meet his gaze, even though she wanted so badly to look away.

The phone started to ring again and Nathan glanced at it. His lips thinned. Alyssa was relieved to be able to look away. She had felt like a butterfly on a pin board.

"Send the text and get that damn thing off." He strode to the armchair and dropped into it.

Alyssa stared at her phone until it fell silent. She quickly typed in, *Heading out of town with friends. Will ring in a week or two*, and sent it before they could ring again. As soon as it came up as sent, she turned off her phone.

"Throw it over here," Nathan said.

Alyssa looked at her phone, then over at Nathan. She shook her head. "I can't. I can't throw."

Nathan looked at her in disbelief. "Too bad. Throw it over. Now."

"I need you to text Erin for a few days. I don't want her to worry yet."

Nathan stared at her for a few minutes before he rose to his feet again. When he stood in front of her, he held out his hand. Alyssa reluctantly handed her phone to him. He turned and threw it so it landed on the armchair. Alyssa held her breath as it bounced and hoped it wouldn't fall off. She looked up at him when the phone came to rest safely on the armchair. He grabbed the handcuff and pulled on her arm so he could snap it onto the frame of the bed head.

"Please, Nathan? It'll benefit you. She won't raise the alarm if she's getting messages from me."

"I'd think you'd want the alarm raised as quickly as possible."

"I'm going to die before dawn, aren't I?" Alyssa was grateful for the numbness that filled her body. It even helped mute the scream.

"Doesn't that bother you?" Nathan frowned.

"You're too fresh in Erin's mind. Give it a few more days and you'll be the last person she'll think of when she no longer receives messages from me."

"Just like that? You accept you're going to die so you'll make sure your friend is protected." Nathan's gaze searched her face. "Have you been planning a suicide?"

Instead of answering and risk he'd hear a lie, Alyssa asked, "Haven't you ever thought of it? Wondered if it might be easier to give up?"

Chapter Five

Nathan shook his head. "Never. I'd fight even against impossible odds. I guess that explains many things. But you're staying chained to the bed. Just because you're willing to die, doesn't mean you'll like our choice of death for you."

"You were going to answer my questions."

"You haven't asked any."

"Why am I here? And don't just tell me to die. Tell me everything. Who am I going to tell? And if I understand it, we have a few hours to fill. I believe I'm stuck here till some time around midnight." Alyssa fought to hold onto the numbness. She needed to learn everything about her situation. Maybe there was something in it she could use to escape. Anything. Hope was sometimes a desperate creature that beat bloody wings against a glass cage while the world outside mocked with its nearness.

Nathan sat on the bed beside her. Once again he stared at her. Alyssa met his gaze steadily. She kept her mind empty and hoped it'd help her achieve the same emotionless look she saw in Nathan's eyes.

"Brian, my father, and I are in property development. A couple of years ago we hired a manager and left the majority of the running in his and the accountant's hands. They had impeccable references. I guess you can't trust anyone these days."

"What has this got to do with me being here?"

"You did tell me you wanted to hear everything. Have you changed your mind?"

Alyssa shook her head. "No."

Nathan stared at her for nearly a full minute and it took all her willpower to remain quiet. Anger started to build as he made her wait and she forced it away. Anger was what had got her in this mess. The numbness was her best chance to get out of it. She forced herself to relax. There'd be nothing gained by trying to hurry Nathan. He liked being in control far too much.

"It's not often we're both fooled. Although I guess when we first hired them, they were exactly as they portrayed themselves. Life can sometimes change people beyond all recognition. I won't go into all the details. But between the two of them, they nearly bankrupted our company while they lined their own pockets. They'll never benefit from their theft." A smile, a mixture of pleasure and cruelty, appeared momentarily. "They left one more problem behind. It's a large piece of land, which if we can change the zoning, will restore our company. But people are too environmentally conscious these days. So we need to call a demon to change their minds for us."

"A what?" Alyssa was certain she couldn't have heard correctly.

"A demon."

"But demon's don't exist."

"Our manager and accountant wouldn't think that. Well, that is if they were alive to think."

Alyssa frantically tried to call back the numbness. As she listened to him speak so calmly of the deaths of others, she wanted to run. And she couldn't. She was handcuffed to the bed. She forced her mind away from thoughts of death and shook her head. "They don't exist."

"Demons are real," Nathan said softly. "My grandfather was the first of us to learn about them. He was an antiques dealer and came across a book on summoning them. He thought it'd be fun. Instead it turned out to be one of his most profitable finds."

"They aren't real."

"Don't you believe in God?"

Alyssa shrugged. "I don't know."

Nathan grinned. "Perfect. The demon we call will be very pleased with you."

"Me?" Her voice came out higher than usual.

"What did you think you were here for? Demons need blood sacrifice to bring them into this world and bind them to the task. Living blood sacrifice. You're the sacrifice."

Alyssa shook her head. "You're crazy, they aren't real."

"They're very real. And you can't conduct business with them without being marked." Nathan undid the button at the cuff of his left sleeve and pulled it back.

A narrow black line with a hint of red in it slashed across his wrist, as if he'd tried to slit it. And yet it was more like a tattoo, or maybe a burn mark. It was part of the skin, not ink added to it. The mark went from the pulse point in the middle of his wrist and travelled to the outside of his arm where it ended abruptly.

"What-" her voice failed her.

"I believe it's known as a demon mark. You have dealings with them that are deep enough, or even frequent, then it appears. Not many people tie themselves so closely to a demon to gain a mark like this. Or come in contact with enough to make such a mark. It took three demons to make it this long." Nathan's fingers traced the mark. "When you ask them to take lives it makes a longer mark. Calling on a powerful demon lengthens it too."

"What… how… the blood sacrifice-"

Nathan's smile didn't reach his eyes. "Have I finally got your attention, little rabbit? Have you taken your head out of the sand to see those headlights coming straight for you?"

Alyssa could only shake her head in disagreement. Words seemed too hard to form. The only word she could hear was demon and it caused all sorts of vivid images to appear in her mind. Ones that involved fire, blood, cloven hooves and horns.

"Surely blood sacrifice is self-explanatory. We need your blood, Allie. We'll cut you so you bleed and use that blood to call the demon. Then you're all his. And the only use he'll have for you is dinner." Nathan's lips curved. "Demons don't feed neatly." His gaze remained on Alyssa.

She refused to give him the reaction he looked for. They hadn't cut her yet. And they wouldn't if she had her way. Her gaze dropped to Nathan's left hand where it rested on his leg. The sleeve had dropped down to hide the demon mark on his wrist. She reached out and lifted the unbuttoned sleeve. Nathan turned his hand so she could see the mark. She ran her fingers over it and wondered if it had hurt. And how had he got it? Had it appeared? Had the demon put it there? She wanted to ask, but the words were lost. She didn't know how to make them form.

"Curious, little rabbit?" Nathan asked softly. "It's such a pity I couldn't replace you. I even got Eric and Shawn to take me for a drive while you slept."

"Aren't you worried they'll tell someone?"

Nathan laughed. "I've got a lot more I can tell someone about them. Some of it much worse than anything they know about me." His tone became serious. "The drive was a waste of time. None of the fish would take the bait. And it has to be tonight. We can't wait."

Startled by his comment, Alyssa's head jerked up and she met his gaze. For a fleeting moment she could have sworn there was regret in them. She dropped her gaze. She didn't want him to see the turmoil in her own. He picked that moment to lean forward and she caught a glimpse of the handcuff key in the pocket of his shirt.

"But don't for one minute think it was due to weakness. You amuse me. But not even for amusement will I risk our company. You're not worth losing out on a billion dollar deal." He whispered the words against her ear where they sounded menacing.

The image of the key that sat in Nathan's pocket was burnt into Alyssa's mind. She could think of only one way to distract him and keep him close to her long enough so she could get it. She turned her head slightly and her lips brushed against his. Her gaze met his and she saw the second of surprise before he willingly took what she offered.

She was surprised it was pleasant. Unlike Tim who she'd dated months ago, it didn't feel like being attacked by an enthusiastic puppy. Nathan knew how to kiss, she'd give him that much. Her hand moved to hover in front of his chest, her gaze focused on his. She'd never kissed anyone with her eyes wide open before and it was disconcerting. Her fingers grazed his shirt and it took all her willpower not to glance down. Her fingers dipped into his pocket and brushed against the cold metal of the key. She caught it between them and started to draw it up and out of the pocket. She nearly had the key out when Nathan's hand pressed hers against his chest and his kiss turned harsh.

Alyssa tried to pull away, but his hand at the nape of her neck prevented her. Without thought, she bit his lip and she felt her eyes widened in surprise as she tasted blood and he jerked away. The hand at her nape tangled tightly in her hair and drew her head back at an awkward angle. Her hand with the key was still trapped against his chest.

"Better than you have tried to distract me, little girl."

"I'm not a little girl."

"I saw your driver's license. Barely eighteen. It takes more than that to become a woman."

"Let me go," Alyssa said through gritted teeth.

"You shouldn't start something if you're not willing to follow through."

"Please." The word was little more than a breath of air. She stared at Nathan, the taste of his blood on her lips and she wished she had a hand free to wipe them clean. Nathan's eyes were expressionless again. She could only wait for his answer. Wait and hope.

He moved forward suddenly, his teeth sharp against her lip. She yelped and tried to pull away. His fingers tightened in her hair. Then he let her go and she fell against the metal bars of the bed head. The fingers of her free hand went to her bottom lip and wiped both her own and his blood from it.

"Now we're even." Nathan rose from the bed.

"They're not real."

"Sure they are, little ostrich. And you'll find out

soon. The demon we call is going to love you. Such sweet blood." He licked his lips.

"No!" She tugged against the handcuffs.

"What's wrong, little rabbit?"

The words stilled her instantly. I won't be a rabbit, she told herself firmly. I won't! She glared at Nathan. There had to be a way out of this mess. So she'd failed at taking the key. There'd be other opportunities. She'd wait for them. "You're crazy if you think killing me will solve your problems."

"Oh it'll solve them all right. Demons are very good at solving problems, if you're careful how you word your demands." He smiled.

Fear rushed through Alyssa and it took all her willpower to remain motionless.

"See. It won't work on you now."

"What won't work?"

"My smile. I asked them to make my smile reassure people. To make them believe what I tell them. I wasn't specific enough. It only works if you want to trust me. If you want to be convinced." Nathan pointed at her. "And last night you wanted to believe. Now you don't. That's why you feel fear when I smile." He smiled momentarily. "But it worked when I needed it to. Now it's another toy to make the game more fun."

Alyssa wished she'd bitten him harder. This wasn't a game. It was her life. "Bastard."

Nathan's reply was another smile. "I'll be back in a few hours. You have a date at three a.m. We can't have you late for that." Nathan strode from the room and let the door swing shut behind him.

Alyssa curled up in a ball at the top of the bed. "Oh God," she moaned. She smothered a laugh. God! If there was any time in her life when prayers were needed, this was it. But not a single one came to mind. She'd never attended church and didn't even know if she'd been baptised. All she could think to say was, "Oh God, help me. If you really exist, I could do with a bit of help about now." When there was no answer to her whispered words, a shudder went through her. "I'm going insane. Believing in demons and gods." She wrapped her free arm across her chest and closed her eyes. There was nothing she could do while handcuffed to the bed. All she could hope for was sleep so the time would pass quicker.

Time! How little there was left. And all the things she hadn't got around to doing. There were so many of them. Alyssa emptied her mind again. She couldn't think. Not without letting a scream escape. It seemed to be getting louder and more insistent. She thought of nothingness. Black, empty nothingness. She wondered if death would be like that. Her breath caught in her throat. She refused to let her mind wander down that track. Instead she started to count. She brought each number to mind in bright red. The colour of blood. Before she reached one hundred, she'd drifted off to sleep again.

Chapter Six

The brush of a finger across her lip brought her to instant wakefulness. Nathan crouched beside the bed. She could only stare at him. Stare and wait to see what move he'd make next.

"Time to get up, Sleeping Beauty. You don't want to be late for your date with a demon."

"I prefer to make an entrance."

Nathan laughed. "An hour and a half till you die and still you make jokes. But don't worry, Princess, as the guest of honour, you'll make an entrance no matter how early you arrive."

As soon as Nathan unlocked the handcuff from her wrist, Alyssa sat up and massaged where it had rubbed against her skin. She yawned and stretched thinking, sleeping too much is as tiring as not sleeping enough. She tried to keep her mind on safe topics. Ones that wouldn't make her scream like a lunatic.

"I need to use the bathroom."

Nathan waved towards the door. Alyssa slung her bag over her shoulder and warily walked towards the open door. She glanced to the left first. The door was closed. She had a feeling that was the way out. She turned right and went straight to the bathroom. As soon as the door was locked, she leaned against it. Time was running out and she didn't have a clue what to do. Her gaze was drawn to the window. She even stood on the toilet seat. It was too small. Far too small. Maybe a child would be able to escape through it, but she couldn't.

She quickly used the toilet and washed her face at the vanity. She stared at herself in the mirror. "Think," she ordered herself. "Think." Her voice broke and she quickly closed her eyes. Maybe it was best not to think. It brought panic closer. She dropped her bag on the vanity and pulled her brush out. She quickly ran it through her hair and then found her makeup. There was no way she'd face death without being as composed as possible. And looking as pale as a ghost wouldn't help her create that image. Makeup would.

There was a knock on the door. "Time's up."

"I haven't finished putting my makeup on."

There was silence for a couple of minutes. "Open the door."

Alyssa glared at the door before she opened it. She stepped back as Nathan entered the tiny room. His gaze went from her face to the makeup strewn on the vanity and then back to her face.

He grinned. "What a waste. If only there'd been another fish to hook." He shrugged. "You have fifteen minutes. If it takes you longer than that, too bad." He shut the door behind him.

Alyssa quickly locked it before she picked up her lipstick. As soon as her makeup was done, she slipped off her boots, and her skirt and pulled on her jeans. Boots were next and then she pushed everything in her handbag and slipped the strap over her head and one arm. She pulled out the water bottle, had a drink and refilled it. Nathan might expect her to die, but she didn't accept she would.

When Alyssa opened the bathroom door, Nathan leaned against the wall. He pushed away from it when she continued to stand there. Without a word, he strode towards the door that had been closed every time she'd looked at it. The one at the end of the hall. He pulled out a key and unlocked it. As he held it open he turned to look at her. Alyssa had to force her feet to move. She wanted to run in the opposite direction. She felt light-headed from lack of food, numb through choice and a scream was desperate to escape.

She stepped through the doorway into a lounge room. An ordinary lounge room. Well, maybe not ordinary. Many people wouldn't have been able to afford the leather lounge or the large flat screen television on the wall. But it was a lounge room, and she hadn't expected to step into something so normal.

She jumped slightly when Nathan closed the door, but continued to face forward. She decided that would be her plan. Not to look back. Nathan brushed past her and headed for a set of French doors on the far side of the room. Alyssa forced herself to follow. Her feet reluctantly obeyed. She wasn't tied and Nathan only seemed to be giving her half his attention. She wanted to keep it that way. Surely there'd be a moment when she could escape. As long as Nathan didn't expect her to try she was sure she had a chance.

Outside they followed a dimly lit path to the front of the house. Nathan opened the door of the car she'd so stupidly climbed into. Even with a demon enhanced smile she should've known better. She hesitated and he pushed at her back so she either had to hop in the car or be pressed against it. The door shut behind her. Alyssa sat quietly and tried to appear relaxed. As Nathan reached for the handle of the driver's door, she carefully pulled on hers. The door moved slightly, just enough she could release the handle and still have the door ready to open. She held her breath. She waited. As soon as Nathan was half in the car, she erupted from her seat, the door slammed shut behind her from the force she shoved it open with.

She heard Nathan swear, but didn't stop. She ran as fast as possible. To the right of the house was what looked like untouched bushland and she aimed straight for it. Maybe she could hide in there. She stumbled on the uneven ground, trying to see where to go in the light cast by the full moon. Everything was outlined in silvery grey, with pockets of shadows to trip the unwary. She reached the tree line, and tried to increase her speed. It was impossible.

She wanted to look behind and see where Nathan was. Instead she reminded herself not to look back. She could hear his feet pound behind her, but she had no idea how far away he was. It became harder to breathe and her lungs burned. Her legs felt like fire, instead of blood, travelled through her veins. She had to find somewhere to hide. And then it was too late.

She felt the impact of Nathan's body before she hit

the ground. His weight kept her pinned. She twisted, tried to toss him off and struck out at him. He fought her, grabbed her hands one at a time and pressed them hard against the earth above her head. She felt sticks and stones dig into her back and side. Her heart continued to pound rapidly, her breath harsh.

"The little ostrich has found her claws," Nathan mocked as soon as she was subdued.

Alyssa stared up at him, a dark shadow that towered over her edged in silver grey. She didn't answer. It was all she could do not to scream. But at least this scream was one of frustration and anger rather than panic. Her breath was harsh in the silence.

"You're patient. I'll give you that much. But you can't escape." Nathan let her go and rose to his feet. "Don't annoy me and I won't track down your friend. If you come quietly she'll be safe. You don't want to mess with me, Princess. I don't make a good enemy. And I like you. So come quietly and I'll make things as easy as possible."

Alyssa sat up and struggled to get to her feet. She ignored the hand Nathan offered her. As soon as she stood, she said, "You must go through a lot of friends then. Their survival rate must be atrocious."

Nathan laughed. "Come on, Princess. You don't want to be late for your date." He draped an arm over her shoulders and she shrugged it off. He put it straight back and tightened his grip on her shoulder when she tried to move away from him.

Alyssa walked stiffly beside Nathan. She wished she could move away from his arm. She felt more confined than she had been by the handcuffs. She knew if she made another attempt to escape she had to succeed. She had no doubt he was serious when he had threatened Erin's life. They'd been best friends forever. There was no way she was going to let Nathan anywhere near Erin.

When they reached the car, Nathan turned Alyssa around and dusted the dirt and leaves from her clothes before he pushed her into the car. "Put your hands on the dash." He stood with the door open and waited for her to follow orders. As soon as her hands were in clear view, he closed the door and walked around to the driver's seat.

Alyssa stared at her hands against the black interior of the car. The moonlight gilded them in silver. Smudges of dirt created dark shadows on her pale fingers. She ignored Nathan as he climbed into the car and only looked over to him when he held her phone out in front of her.

"Save five messages I can send to your friend. I

won't send them in any particular order so keep that in mind."

Alyssa's fingers closed over the phone. For a split second she considered sending a plea for help instead of saving drafts to say she was safe. But she didn't know where she was. There was no information she could pass along. Not without endangering those she loved. She turned on the phone and ignored the voice messages that needed to be listened to. They were probably all from her parents. Thoughts of her mother made her fingers fly across the buttons. She wanted to get her phone turned off before she tried to ring again.

While Alyssa wrote messages for Erin, she sent glances towards Nathan as he turned the car around and drove towards the road at the end of a long curved driveway. He turned right onto it and pressed his foot hard on the accelerator. Alyssa was jolted back in her seat as the car responded. She started to check the speed he was doing and then wondered why it mattered. Death by car accident or death by demon. She had a feeling the car accident would be the easiest.

Messages written, Alyssa worried at her bottom lip with her teeth. She ignored the small pain the cut caused. Only the living feel pain, she reminded herself. She stared at Nathan. She didn't want to ask anything of him. But what choice did she have? This might be the end. A strange sense of calm settled over her and she wondered if she'd remain calm right through to the end. She didn't think so. She guessed it was probably shock and her brain unable to process any more details.

"What?" Nathan glanced over at her when she continued to watch him.

"If I leave a message for my parents will you send it to them on the sixth day?"

"Depends on what it says."

"Nothing to connect us."

"Write it and I'll think about it."

Alyssa wanted to demand he send it. She knew that'd cause him to do the opposite. Instead she looked at the tiny screen that blurred. She blinked. She refused to cry. She forced herself to write the message, not knowing how much time she had left.

"Read it out." Nathan slowed the vehicle and turned onto a dirt track.

Alyssa gathered the numbness to her again. In a voice barely above a whisper, she said, "I'm sorry for everything. I didn't mean for things to go the way they did. I love you both. You aren't to blame for the mess I made. I wish I knew what else to say. Goodbye seems inadequate."

Silence filled the vehicle. Alyssa turned the phone off and automatically slipped it into the outside pocket of her handbag. She looked out the window. She didn't want to see if her words amused Nathan. She saw a flicker of light through the gum trees. Fire. Her heart felt like it stopped beating for a few seconds before it started again at a gallop. She guessed they were nearly there.

Chapter Seven

Nathan stopped the car at the edge of a clearing beside another vehicle, this one a four-wheel-drive. She sat quietly in her seat as Nathan came around and opened her door. He waited for her to move. When she didn't, he reached in and grabbed her arm to pull her out.

"Don't be uncooperative."

Alyssa remained silent. She glanced around. A man stood near a flickering fire that was surrounded by rocks to contain it. He looked like an older version of Nathan and Alyssa guessed this was Brian. His hair was cropped short with a hint of silver in the sides and he had a neat moustache. He wore a business suit as if he attended a meeting and Alyssa battled the bubble of hysteria that threatened to escape. About fifteen metres from where Brian stood was a wooden stake standing two metres out of the ground.

Alyssa stopped when she realised this was where Nathan was headed. He gripped her arm tightly and tugged her along with him. Her mouth dried and she had to fight the scream that clawed to escape. She didn't know why she held it in. This was the end and there was no one here but Nathan and his father to see how she reacted. Anger coursed through her. How dare they do this? She wanted to strike out at them. She wanted to make them hurt. Bleed. But instead she was being helplessly led to her death.

Nathan turned her so her back was to the stake and picked up a length of rope lying on the ground beside it. He lifted her hands above her head and tied them to a metal ring set towards the top of the stake. There was no way to escape from these bonds. They were as unbreakable as the handcuffs had been.

Nathan stayed close. "No kiss goodbye?"

Alyssa forced herself to smile. "Only if you're willing to pay the price." She snapped her teeth to make sure he understood.

"I know you're faking it. I can see your pulse beat as rapidly as a hummingbird's wing." Nathan pressed his fingers against her throat.

"Do you believe in ghosts?"

Nathan frowned.

"I'm going to haunt you till the day you die. In

fact you're going to wish yourself dead. I'm going to make you want to kill yourself."

"Never."

"Your life's going to become pure torture. Revenge will be so sweet." Alyssa mimicked the cruel smile she'd seen on Nathan. She wished with her whole heart this was possible. If she had to die here she wanted to have some way to make him pay.

"I think not. The demon will take your soul. Then there'll be nothing of you to haunt me."

"My soul is my own and I give it to no one."

"You say that now. But before the demon's finished with you, the pain'll be so great you'll offer it to him in exchange for ending it quick. I've seen it before."

"When have I ever done as you expected? Every bit of pain I feel, I'll imagine you feeling it ten times over. I'll relish it. I'll see you soon, Nathan. Maybe then I'll give you a kiss hello." Alyssa's smile widened at the look of uncertainty that flickered across Nathan's face. She didn't know where the inspiration had come from, could only put it down to desperation. "That doesn't interest you? I'm hurt." She pouted theatrically then laughed. She'd have preferred to yell in triumph at the seed of doubt she'd sown in Nathan's mind, but she didn't want to overplay her hand.

"You're mad," Nathan whispered.

"No. You're the one who's mad, Nathan. Who invited me to come and play with demons? Surely you didn't think I'd play by your rules. I'm not much for rules. Why else would I have been crazy enough to get into your car?"

"Nathan! What's taking so long? It's getting close to three."

Nathan turned at the interruption. "One minute, Brian." He faced Alyssa. "You will not become a ghost. And you will not return to haunt me." He stressed the word 'not' each time he said it.

Alyssa's smile never faltered. "I swear it on the blood you spill. If I die tonight I'll haunt you till you beg for death."

"Nathan!" His father bellowed impatiently.

"Then I guess we'll see who's stronger." Nathan bent and picked up a knife and goblet from the ground beside the stake. "Time to scream, little rabbit."

Alyssa was glad for the warning. She clenched her teeth against the burning fire each shallow cut he made on her arms caused. She felt the blood drip. She blocked the sensation from her mind, her gaze focused on Nathan. She burnt his image into her mind. His boyish, smooth shaved face and narrow chin. Brown eyes and black hair that was normally neatly styled, but was messed from their earlier struggles. Narrow nose, thick brows and a lack of expression other than the occasional wry amusement. If she could come back, she'd be able to find him anywhere. She ignored the cold metal of the goblet as it was pressed against her arms to catch her blood.

"Well done, little rabbit." Nathan met her gaze. He paused. "Don't be foolish, Allie. Let it end quick. Tell him your soul for a quick death. That's all it'll take for it to be over in seconds."

"I'll see you later, Nathan."

Nathan swore.

"What? Regrets, Nathan?"

"We all do what we must in life."

"How true. In that case, I won't say goodbye."

Nathan swore again before he turned and strode towards his father, the goblet in his hand, the knife at her feet. She watched as Brian took a bowl from the ground and sprinkled something white to create a circle around them. He put the bowl on the ground and she saw his lips move and wondered what he said. He looked like he chanted, but the quiet words didn't travel to her, only a low hum of sound.

I never did try and pick the lock of the handcuffs, Alyssa thought. I wonder if it would've worked? I hope he sends the texts. I didn't give him my phone. Will he get it from my bag when I'm gone? The random thoughts tumbled through her mind. She'd expected the end to be more. Where were all the flashes of memory people spoke of? Had her life been so forgettable? She hadn't thought so. Alyssa flinched as Brian's voice rose.

"Come! I name you Retribution!" He poured her blood from the goblet and it sprinkled the ground outside his circle. "I offer you living sacrifice in exchange for the safety of me and mine and a favour."

The ground began to shift like it was melting. A shape pressed up out of the dirt. Then it seemed as if fire burst forth like a fountain. It solidified into an almost human shape. That is if a human had wings, horns on its head and was red in colour. Not a solid red like Alyssa had expected, more like lava flowing with its movement and shadows. Then he turned and faced her and all resemblance to a human body builder with wings evaporated. The face was a grotesque mask of evil, eyes a deep black like bottomless pits of hell in the fiery red.

Alyssa finally opened her mouth to scream. But it was too late. Fear had frozen her vocal chords and she was unable to make a sound. The demon moved towards her. He didn't walk, nor did he glide. He seemed to grow closer the longer she stared at him. Her whole body trembled and if she hadn't been tied to the stake she would've been a boneless puddle on the ground.

The demon stopped in front of her. He ran his hand down her left arm, blood coating his fingers. The burning pain of his touch made the world around Alyssa swim out of focus. If his touch caused this much pain, how was she going to manage when he deliberately caused pain? She had to hold onto her soul. It was her last hope. Not exactly an escape, but not giving in either.

The demon raised his fingers to his mouth and licked her blood from them. His body seem to pulse or flare like a fire that had been fed more timber and Alyssa gasped as pain exploded through her. The demon turned towards Nathan and his father. Sweat beaded across Alyssa's brow and lip as heat emanated from the demon. The smell of him burnt the back of her throat. Like bushfires, metal and rotten eggs all at once. Her pain started to subside.

"I am yours to command. Retribution will be my name." His voice seemed to be everywhere at once. You could not tell which direction it came from. He turned to face Alyssa.

She tried to close her eyes. She didn't want to

see the end. But the twin pools of hell mesmerised her and she was unable to look away. The demon reached up and snapped the bonds that held her to the stake. She dropped, landing at his feet. Her right hand closed over the knife coated with her blood. She didn't know what she could do with it, but it was better than going peacefully.

The demon grabbed her by her hair and dragged her upright. Alyssa struck, amazed at how easy the knife entered him. He let her go with a roar. Alyssa hit the ground hard. She looked up through her hair to see the demon rip the knife from his torso and fling it to the ground.

The sounds of a fast moving vehicle and lights flickering through the gum trees caught Alyssa's attention and she missed seeing the demon strike out at her. She sprawled backwards and her face felt like it was on fire. Pain radiated through her entire body. She heard car doors slam and Nathan's father bellow in rage. She tried to focus. But her head spun and her ears had a faint buzzing sound in them. She blinked. At an angle to her a young woman faced the demon. She was slim with wiry muscles that held a long sword effortlessly in two hands. She wore black denim jeans, a black singlet edged with lace and sensible boots. The only jewellery she wore was a small gold cross on a leather necklace resting on the pulse at her throat. Her blond hair was cut short to feather around her face, adding to the pixyish look her fine boned face gave her. She glanced down at Alyssa before she turned her gaze back to the demon. Alyssa had an impression of warm brown eyes that brimmed with the many emotions Nathan's had lacked.

Alyssa wondered if she was hallucinating. The young woman seemed like a modern day angel minus the wings. Alyssa could think of no one else who'd stand before a demon with only a sword. The woman advanced. Her lips moved and the demon retreated. Alyssa heard the sound of gunfire and Nathan and his father yell abuse at someone. She struggled to get to her feet. She needed to see what was happening. Finding that an impossible task, she crawled to the knife and wrapped her fingers around the handle. She turned back in the direction she had come from and froze.

A young man dressed similar to the sword wielding woman crouched beside her. The only difference was he wore a t-shirt instead of a singlet. Alyssa cringed back from him, wary of his handsome face. His sandy blond hair was short at the back and sides with a little more length at the front. He had the same warm brown eyes as the woman and wore a silver stud in the shape of a cross in one ear. He also wore the same necklace as the woman. A sword rested in a scabbard on his back.

He smiled at Alyssa and held his hand out to her in greeting. "Riley Hunter. That's my cousin Scarlett Hunter. Looks like you could do with a bit of help."

Alyssa could only stare at him. Maybe this was a hallucination due to blood loss. Her gaze was drawn to the blood that trickled down her arms. How much could you lose before it was too much? And she was pretty sure some of it wasn't hers, but it was impossible to know how much belonged to the demon. She looked back towards Riley. His hand remained outstretched. A look of compassion filled his eyes.

"What's your name, sweetheart?"

Another gunshot had her turning her head nervously towards the sound. She heard Nathan swear again. She really needed to see what was happening. She looked at Riley. She started to reach out to take his hand then stopped. It seemed too convenient. How had they known to come here at this moment?

"How about we try a different question? Do you believe in God?"

Alyssa was startled by the question. She opened her mouth to answer, but didn't know what to say. Did she? A couple of days ago she'd have said no. But then she'd also have said demons didn't exist. And why was she even thinking about answering his questions. She had to run. But would he follow?

"Well, that makes it a bit trickier," Riley said softly. "Know any prayers?" When Alyssa shook her head, he sighed, but his smile barely wavered. "Ah well, a challenge is always good for one's character. At least that's what Gran keeps telling me."

Alyssa shook her head in disbelief. Riley sat in front of her and talked about his Gran as if they'd met at a party. His cousin faced a demon a few metres away and he didn't seem in the least concerned. With each hour that passed her life became more surreal.

"Come on, love. Let me help you up and we'll get you out of here." Riley continued to hold out his hand.

"Stop being so nice, Riley."

Alyssa scrambled away, trying to see both Riley and the person behind her. This young man didn't have the charming, boy-next-door looks of Riley. His dark brown hair was cut so short as to almost be shaved. He had a square jaw, sharp cheekbones, deep brown eyes and a solemn look. He had broader shoulders than Riley and held his sword ready, his feet planted firmly apart for balance.

"That's Scarlett's brother, Alex. My cousin. Don't mind him. He's always cranky," Riley said.

"It's not a tea party, Riley. Grab the girl and let's get out of here."

"Allie!" Alyssa jerked at Nathan's shout. "Damn you, Allie! I'm going to track your friend down!"

"Allie? Is that you?" When Alyssa continued to stare at him, Riley asked, "Is that short for Alison?"

Alyssa shook her head. She scrambled back a bit further from the two young men, her handbag bumping against her hip. She had to get away from here. Had to get away from all of them.

"Come on, Riley. Grab her and get her in the vehicle. We've got to be ready to go the moment dawn hits the sky. Those two aren't going to stay in their circle of power one second longer than they have to." Alex slid his sword in his scabbard.

"She's scared, Alex."

"Better scared than dead." Alex strode towards Alyssa and she cringed away from him. But it wasn't enough. He twisted the knife from her hand, gave it to Riley and threw her over his shoulder. Alyssa exploded into action. She kicked, hit and tried to throw herself to the ground.

Alex strode towards their four-wheel-drive and occasionally staggered under her onslaught. "Keep that demon headed away from the vehicle, Scarlett. Help her, Riley," Alex ordered as he dumped Alyssa on the ground by the vehicle.

"That's it, Allie," Nathan called from where he stood by his father, unable to leave the circle of power. Brian stood beside him, a gun clutched in his hand. "You fight him, Princess. You don't want to go with them. You've got a job to complete. Remember sweet little Erin? And what about your parents? I know where you live, Allie."

Chapter Eight

Alyssa grabbed hold of the vehicle and pulled herself to her feet. Anger coursed through her. She started to move towards Nathan. She didn't know what she'd do to him. But she wanted to make him hurt. Hurt as much as he'd made her hurt. When Alex grabbed her arm, she tried to push him away.

"Let me go," she snarled.

Alex pulled her close, his expression fierce. "We won't let him get them. We can protect them."

"I don't know you. Why should I trust you?"

"I swear to God we'll protect them. With our own lives. You have to trust someone, Allie."

"Why are you here?"

"Our Gran sent us. She saw you were in trouble. Her visions are a little imprecise before the fact. As well as rare. But when she has them, they become clearer closer to the event."

"What? She's a clairvoyant?" Alyssa laughed in disbelief.

Alex shook his head. "No. We're demon hunters. She's only sent visions to help find demons."

"And your last name's hunter? You must think me an idiot."

Alex smiled for the first time. A wry hint that was quickly gone. "I keep telling the family we should change our name. It undermines our credibility. But we've held the name and task for centuries. I guess most of us are a stubborn lot."

"Undermines your credibility?" Alyssa stared at him. He stood there telling her his family had made a career hunting demons and he expected her to believe he was worried their surname undermined their credibility.

"Don't tease, Alex," Scarlett said from a couple of metres away, still holding the demon at bay with her sword. She glanced skyward. "Any minute now."

"Hop in the vehicle, Allie." Alex put his left hand on her shoulder as he spoke.

Alyssa's gaze was drawn to the thin lines that started at his pulse and snaked around his wrist nearly three times. "Demon marks." She pulled away from him, her retreat prevented by the vehicle, items from her handbag digging into her lower back.

"I told you we're demon hunters. You think that doesn't mark you? Coming into contact with a demon marks everyone. Even you." Alex reached forward and grabbed a lock of her hair. He pulled it forward for her to see.

Alyssa's mouth dropped open at the blood red lock that had once been purple. "No," she snatched it from his fingers, clasping it tight. "I hate this colour."

Alex's hand closed over hers. He pried her fingers apart and brushed her hair back from her face with the other. "It won't take dye. You're stuck with this streak for life. A souvenir."

Alyssa shook her head. Her vision blurred and her throat started to ache from trying to control her emotions for so long. "No." The word was nearly soundless.

"Run!" Scarlett screamed.

Alyssa had no chance to react. Alex shoved her in the vehicle and slammed the door behind her. Riley was seated beside her in seconds and grabbed hold of her hands as they went for the door handle. His sword leaned against the seat between them. Scarlett and Alex hopped into the front almost simultaneously, their swords landing on Riley's. Alex had the vehicle in motion before the front doors were shut. Alyssa glanced out the window to see Nathan and Brian run past Nathan's sedan to the four-wheel-drive. Brian stopped to reload his gun and Alyssa shuddered as she saw Nathan mouth the word Erin. She tried to pull her hands from Riley, but he wouldn't let her.

"Let me go! I've got to ring Erin."

"What are you going to tell her?" Scarlett turned in her seat to look at Alyssa.

"He can't get her. Let me go!" She bent forward to use her teeth, but Riley let go.

"Put your seat belt on, Allie," Alex said calmly.

Alyssa glanced around at the other three and realised they all had their seat belts on. She was about to argue, but a sharp corner threw her against Riley and the swords shifted towards him. She hurriedly drew away from him and buckled up. Riley gathered the swords and laid them across the floor at their feet.

"Give me her full name and address and we'll have people keep her safe." Scarlett pulled a phone from her pocket.

"I don't know you people!" Alyssa yelled the words before she dropped her head in her hands and shook it from side to side.

"We can take you to people who'll vouch for us. What about the priest of our church?" Riley reached out to pat Alyssa's shoulder.

She jerked away and glared at him. "I don't know your priest."

"I doubt we'd move in the same circles, Ry." Scarlett shrugged. "If she doesn't want to trust us, there's nothing we can do for her."

Alex swung on the steering wheel and Alyssa swore as she was thrown against the door.

"Not around us, Allie," Scarlett said.

"What?"

"No swearing. You can sin all you want away from us, but not while you're with us. Demons are hard enough to battle without that stain." Scarlett slipped her phone in her pocket.

"You're kidding." Alyssa looked from one to the other. They all looked serious.

Riley grabbed a backpack off the floor and took a bottle of water from it. "We're deadly serious." He took a mouthful and then offered it to Alyssa who shook her head.

"I don't suppose you've got food in there," Alyssa asked.

Riley handed her the backpack. "Help yourself."

Alyssa looked inside and nearly shouted in relief. Breakfast bars, chocolate, chips, jerky, lollies, savoury and sweet biscuits, mini cheese and fruit. She took out some crackers, cheese, fruit and chocolate before she returned the backpack.

"How long since you've eaten?" Scarlett asked.

Alyssa frowned.

"That's what I thought," Scarlett said. "Only have a couple of crackers for now. I'm not having you throw up in here."

"And with the way Alex drives that's always a possibility," Riley said as Alex took another corner fast.

Alyssa glared at Scarlett. She didn't want to listen to her words. She wanted to eat every bit of food that sat in her lap and then raid the backpack for more. When she would've opened the chocolate, Riley covered her hands with his. Alyssa looked up at him and wanted to look away the moment she saw the pity in his eyes. She moved her hands away from him and he retreated.

"Put it in your bag for later. Trust me, it won't be half so pleasant coming back up as it is going down," Riley said.

"Riley!"

Riley grinned at Scarlett's look of disgust. "Well it won't."

Alex took another corner hard and Scarlett turned

her attention to her brother. "How about we get there in one piece, little brother."

"Little brother?" Alyssa was startled by Scarlett's comment.

Scarlet chuckled. "I know he's not so little at six foot, but he's the youngest of us." Alyssa glanced towards Riley, which caused Scarlett to laugh. "He's the oldest. Riley's twenty, I'm nineteen and Alex is eighteen. Riley has a brother, Blake, who's twenty-two. So I guess we could always put it down to him being the baby in his family."

"Twenty?" Alyssa asked incredulously. "I thought he was my age."

"Hey, if I didn't joke around, it'd be as somber as a grave around you lot. Just because we're demon hunters doesn't mean we have to act like death's always imminent." Riley grinned. "Even if it is."

Alyssa popped a cracker in her mouth and looked out the window. She tried to remind herself the people in the vehicle with her were strangers. But there'd been moments when she felt like she knew them. She absently shoved the food in her bag as she tried to get her bearings. She kept out a handful of crackers. She sat up straight, as she realised where they were. "We're going into the city. Why?"

"Good place to lose a tail." Alex glanced up in the rear view mirror.

Alyssa looked out the back window and her heart started to race again. Her body began to tremble and she forced herself to turn forward.

Riley reached out to her and patted her hand. "We won't let him get you."

Alyssa started to push his hand away. Instead she turned it so she could examine his demon mark. It didn't quite go twice around his wrist. She was surprised at how evenly the line was as it snaked around. The same diameter, the same spacing. She glanced towards Alex then back at Riley's wrist. "They're different lengths."

"We don't always work together. Demons have different levels of power. Scarlett's mark is the same length as mine," Riley said.

Alyssa looked over to Scarlet who held up her wrist to show her. "Does it hurt? When it appears. Or whatever it does." Alyssa ran her fingers over the smooth skin of Riley's wrist.

It was Riley who drew away this time. "Not really. A slight burning sensation. You can watch it being drawn. I guess that's the best description."

Alyssa glanced at her wrist. "Why don't I have one?"

"Because you haven't linked yourself to him properly. Either to summon or send him on his way," Riley said.

"Gather belongings." Alex turned into a multilevel parking lot. Within seconds of pulling up at the gate, it was opening and letting them through.

"What are we doing?" Alyssa demanded. "Why are we in here?"

"Vehicle swap," Scarlett said. She handed a dark blanket to Alyssa. "Put this around you in case there's someone about when we stop. You look like you've been tortured."

Alyssa looked at her blood streaked arms. She glanced up when Riley handed her a couple of baby wipes. "What do I need these for?"

"Your face is covered in blood. You want me to clean it off for you?"

Alyssa shook her head as she took the moist wipes. "It's not all mine."

Scarlett handed her a small plastic bag. "Whose blood is it?"

Alyssa dropped the rust coloured wipes into the small plastic bag. "The demon's." When Scarlett remained quiet, she asked, "Is that a problem?"

Riley handed her more wipes. "Not exactly. Just

don't be surprised if your wounds heal quicker than usual."

"Any minute now," Alex said. "Hope you're all ready."

They drove up several levels and Alex pulled into a reserved parking spot near an elevator. The other three were out of the vehicle before Alyssa was halfway out and Scarlett hurried her out of the way so she could shut the door. Riley was already at the elevator, waiting for it to arrive. They each carried a backpack and their sheathed sword. Alyssa dropped her bag of rubbish into a bin by the elevator.

"Hurry." Riley urged Alyssa inside the elevator the moment the doors slid open. As soon as they were all in, he hit each number from four to seven.

"Why?" Alyssa looked at the number panel.

"So they don't know which level we get off." Riley pulled a bright button up shirt out of his backpack and a cap. The shirt he threw on and left unbuttoned, the cap he put on backwards.

Alyssa watched Scarlett drop a coffee coloured long dress on over her clothes and a thin straw hat on her head. Alex now wore a bright shirt like Riley's, had a mop of dark curls and dark sunglasses. Alyssa opened her mouth to ask what was going on when the elevator door opened. Riley put his arm around her shoulders and the four of them stepped out onto level five.

Alex had another set of keys in his hand and pushed the central locking for a navy coloured sedan two bays away from the elevator. Riley pushed Alyssa into the car and onto the floor. His backpack and sword went in too and he shut the door.

"There they go," Scarlett murmured from the front passenger seat as Alex started the car.

"Who? Nathan and Brian?" Alyssa was about to sit up, but Riley pushed her down as he hopped into the car.

"Are you mad?" Scarlett hissed.

Alyssa frowned. "You know, I probably am. This is all a psychotic episode. I forgot to take my pills. I'm going to remember to take them in future."

Riley laughed as he buckled up. "Hang onto that sense of humour. You're going to need it until we can get rid of the demon."

"I wasn't trying to be funny. Where are we going now?" Alyssa demanded as she felt Alex reverse out of the car park.

"As soon as we've made sure the wolf isn't following, we're off to Grandma's house." Riley grinned down at her.

"You're not in the least bit amusing," Alyssa muttered.

"We tell him that all the time, but it doesn't seem to stop him," Scarlett said.

Alex exited the car park and waited until they were a block away before he said, "You can hop up now. And Riley was telling the truth. We're going to our Gran's house. It's where we live." He pulled off the wig and dropped it beside him.

Alyssa left the blanket on the floor as she slid onto the seat and buckled up. "I don't know your Gran. I just want to go home."

"Looking like that?" Scarlett turned in her seat.

"A few more baby wipes and I'll be fine," Alyssa said.

Riley pulled a first aid kit from his backpack and sat it on the seat between them. "Give me a few minutes and you won't look half as bad, sweetheart."

"No. I'll do it myself." Alyssa reached out to the first aid kit, but Riley put his hand on the lid. She looked up at him, about to argue. It was the first time she'd seen him when he wasn't already smiling or looked like he was about to smile.

"I know you've had a tough time. And I'm sure you're wary of everyone. But answer me one little question, love. Have we done anything since you've met us to warrant this distrust?" Riley stared at her as he waited patiently for her answer.

Uncomfortable, Alyssa looked away. "Nathan-"

Riley interrupted, "I didn't ask about anyone other than us. Don't put the sins of others on our shoulders."

The silence stretched out, but Alyssa knew there was only one answer she could give. "No."

"Then let me clean and dress your wounds. You can't do it properly yourself."

Alyssa finally nodded and Riley opened the first aid kit. He took her right arm and turned it so he could clean the wounds, first with the baby wipes and then with antiseptic. Once the cuts were clean, he pulled out an Elastoplast roll and cut enough at the correct length for the cut on each arm. As soon as that arm was finished, he leaned across her to deal with the other.

Riley returned everything to the first aid kit and grinned. "That wasn't so bad now was it, sweetheart?"

Alyssa shrugged. "I'm not your sweetheart."

Riley laughed. "And not very sweet at the moment either."

Chapter Nine

Alyssa turned away, ignoring the soft laughter from the front of the car. She took her phone out and sent one of her saved messages to Erin. She wanted to ring her and warn her. But how could she explain a demon was out for her blood and a lunatic would be trying to use Erin as an incentive to let the demon kill her. The only people she had to turn to for help were those in the car with her. She glanced out the window. The houses they drove past were a blur. She really had no choice. Erin's life was in danger. Even her parents were at risk. She looked over to Scarlett who was scribbling in a notebook. Next she pulled a small laptop from her backpack and turned it on.

"Scarlett?" Alyssa waited for Scarlett to twist in her seat to face her. "Can you have someone look out for my friend and parents?"

"Of course. I just need to know details." Scarlett

opened up her email account and quickly typed up an email with the details Alyssa gave her. Within minutes she had a reply. "Done."

"Just like that?" Alyssa stared at Scarlett, her gaze drawn momentarily to the computer screen.

Scarlett laughed. "Yeah, just like that."

"We've been doing this for centuries. Don't you think we'd be at least a little organised?" Riley asked.

"We?" Alyssa asked hesitantly.

"Our family. Some people tend to have doctors or lawyers in the family. We have demon hunters." Riley grinned. "A much more interesting career choice."

"I can't think it'd be a very profitable business to be in," Alyssa said.

The three demon hunters laughed. It was Alex who answered. "It's a good thing we don't rely on it for an income then."

Alyssa wanted to ask what they did rely on for an income, but couldn't bring herself to. She cast around for another topic to discuss, but could think of nothing. So she sat in silence and stared out the window. She didn't have a clue where she was. None of the streets seemed familiar. It looked like an upmarket suburb, with large houses, spacious blocks of land and many of the driveways had more than one vehicle in them. She saw families pile into vans and four-wheel-drives to head out for the day. She imagined they were going to the beach before the workweek started tomorrow. Work! She was meant to be at work on Monday from nine o'clock until midday. And each day until Friday. She didn't know how she could accomplish that. All she wanted to do was hide away from the world and forget every second that had occurred since she'd left Erin standing on the side of the road.

"Home sweet home." Riley interrupted Alyssa's thoughts.

She looked at the spacious house nestled in a riot of flowering gardens. It was made of timber painted in neutral creams and browns and white backed curtains hung at the windows. They pulled up in front of closed double garage doors.

Riley bounded out of the car with his sword and backpack and called over his shoulder, "I'll see about breakfast."

"It's nearly ten. How about brunch?" Scarlett said, only a few steps behind him.

Alyssa continued to sit in the car, as Alex climbed out of the driver's seat and walked around to her door and opened it. He leaned forward, one arm braced on the door pillar and the other held the door. His sword and backpack sat at his feet. He solemnly watched her.

Alyssa looked up at him and then away. She pulled her handbag closer, glanced up at Alex again and then looked straight ahead. Words and phrases drifted through her mind. She finally settled on one she could speak. "Why am I here?"

"To regroup and plan our next step."

Alyssa, startled by his answer, met his gaze. She found it hard to believe he was her age. He seemed far older. Even his eyes looked like they should belong to a man a good ten to fifteen years older. She wondered what experiences had given him that look. "But… didn't… the demon-" A shudder coursed through her and she couldn't continue.

Alex held out the hand that had been holding the car door. "Come inside. You don't have to see any of my family. There's a lounge room just off the entrance hall. You can be alone in there."

Alyssa looked at his hand warily. "How many will be inside?"

"I don't know. It varies. Usually no more than twenty. But we've been known to have three times that many here during large operations. And celebrations."

Alyssa hesitantly took Alex's hand and let him draw

her out of the car. She was relieved he let her hand go the moment she was out. She adjusted her handbag strap so it lay more comfortably across her chest and shoulder. She was amazed she still had it. Alex took a step away from her. She was glad it was Alex who'd stayed outside with her. He might be more intense than the other two, but she felt safer and relaxed with him. His serious expression made her think he was someone who could be counted on in a crisis. She guessed they all could be, after all, what could be worse than facing demons?

Alex gestured towards the front door. "The lounge room?"

Alyssa nodded. She guessed she had to do something. It wasn't like she could stand by the car all day. As soon as she nodded, Alex walked to the front door and held it open for her. When she was inside, he opened a door on the right of the entrance hall. She glanced around. There were two closed doors on her left and a door straight ahead. On either side of the front door were racks hung with coats and hats and wooden boxes with a jumble of shoes.

"Allie? Did you want to go somewhere else instead?"

Alyssa quickly shook her head and crossed the off-white tiles to enter the lounge room. A pale brown lounge suite was scattered in the middle of the room with a rustic coffee table and a couple of large footstools. Pictures of what Alyssa guessed were family members hung in groups on the walls and there was a long display cabinet filled with ornaments along one wall. Opposite the door the wall was taken up by floor to ceiling bookcases with glass doors. To her right a large window spilled light into the room.

"Have a seat. Make yourself comfortable."

Alyssa worried at her lower lip with her teeth. "I can't. I'll make a mess of them. I need to wash."

"They can be cleaned. But if it bothers you, there are throw rugs in the footstools."

Alyssa felt like asking Alex how dense he was. Her cheeks coloured at the thought of having to ask him to use the toilet. And the blood. She had to get rid of the blood. She continued to worry at her bottom lip.

"The door across from this one in the entrance hall is a bathroom. If you want to have a wash, I'll organise a change of clothes for you. There's a bathrobe behind the door you can use and towels in the cupboard just inside the door."

"Thanks." Alyssa stepped back into the entrance hall. She was in the bathroom in seconds, the door closed and locked. The off-white and cream colour scheme was in the bathroom too, but they had also added a few touches of gold. When Alyssa saw the bathtub, her eyes watered and she slid to the floor. She rested her head against the door, eyes closed as she desperately tried to hold on a little longer. The pressure of her bladder soon had her rising to her feet to use the toilet.

While she was on her feet, she started to run a bath, grabbed a towel from the cupboard and ditched her handbag, clothes and bandaids in a pile on the floor. She quickly hopped in and closed her eyes, sinking beneath the water. When she came up, she gasped at the colour of the water. She frantically searched for the plug. Her hands trembled so badly she could barely pull it. She watched as the discoloured water slowly drained away. Sitting in the tub as the water continued to run she could only shiver uncontrollably as silent tears ran down her face. She tried to force herself to move, but the sight of the blood coloured water had been too much. She rocked back and forth and tried desperately not to have a complete break down.

A sharp knock on the bathroom door caused fear to rush through her. She turned her head, her gaze glued to the door. She couldn't move. You're safe, you idiot. But her limbs remained frozen. Her body didn't believe her.

"Allie?" When she didn't answer, Alex asked, "You want me to get Scarlett?"

"No!" The word exploded from her.

"I've put clothes in the room next door to the bathroom for you. I'll be in the lounge room when you're finished."

"Okay." She waited. She strained her ears for the sound of footsteps, but heard none. Surely he wasn't still out there. She rose shakily to her feet and turned on the shower. She kept sending glances towards the door.

As soon as no more blood showed in the water around her feet, Alyssa turned off the taps and climbed out of the tub. She dried herself, wrapped her hair with the towel and pulled on the bathrobe. She caught a glimpse of her face in the mirror. Her fingers hesitantly touched the bruise from where the demon had struck her. She swallowed hard and looked away, her gaze falling on the closed door. She took one step towards it and froze. Annoyance rushed through her.

You never used to jump at shadows, she reminded herself. That was before I knew they could jump out at me. Well it's daylight now. The sun obviously scares away shadows. Only the mythical ones. Are you going to let them turn you into a cowering mess?

What happened to the girl who was going to haunt Nathan? Are you a little rabbit?

Alyssa groaned and closed her eyes. "Now I'm arguing with myself." She shook her head and then had to steady the towel she nearly dislodged. "One step at a time." She picked her boots up off the floor, grabbed her handbag and forced herself to open the bathroom door. The entrance hall was empty. She scurried to the door beside the bathroom and flung it open.

A bedroom with the same colour scheme met her gaze. The only colours other than cream was a pale copper bedspread on the queen-sized bed and the warm tones of the two timber bedside cabinets and the duchess that stood against the wall near the door. As soon as she'd closed and locked the bedroom door, Alyssa picked up the clothes on the bed. Black jeans, black t-shirt, underwear and socks.

As she dressed, she wondered who the clothes belonged to. Scarlett was slightly slimmer and a little taller than her so these clothes couldn't be hers. Unless they were ones she used to fit. Then she recalled the other sixty or more people that frequented the house. She shrugged. The clothes could belong to anyone. She was just glad she didn't have to wear her bloodstained ones. But then if these clothes belong to someone else, it brought to mind another question. She quickly towel dried her hair and then returned the towel to the bathroom, ignoring the mess she couldn't face. She paused by the two boxes of shoes at the front door and reluctantly left her boots leaned up against one of them. As she slung the strap of her bag over her head and put one arm through it she stepped into the lounge room.

"Why do you all wear black?"

Alex rose to his feet and placed the hardcover book he was reading face down on the coffee table. "You're looking a lot better. How do you feel?"

"Okay."

"I'll get you new bandaids."

Alyssa shook her head. "The cuts have stopped bleeding."

"Come and sit down and I'll find you something to eat."

Alyssa stepped further into the room. "Why do you all wear black clothes?"

Alex stared at her quietly for a moment. "They're less likely to show up bloodstains."

"Oh." Alex stepped forward to take her arm, but she pulled away. "I'm not an invalid."

"I know."

She strode to an armchair and sat on the edge of

it as she glanced at the book on the coffee table. She froze, her breath drawn in sharply when she saw the picture of the demon on the cover. Alex reached for the book. Her hand landed on it first as she tried to tell herself it was only a picture. Not the real thing. She was safe. Her gaze rose to meet his.

He stared at her for a moment before he stepped back. "No need to save my place, I've read it many times." He paused. "I'll get you something to eat." He left the room before Alyssa could speak.

She picked up the book and closed it to stare at the front cover. 'Demonology' by Patrick Hunter. She turned a couple of pages and the inscription caught her eye. "So it is said that if you know your enemies and know yourself, you will fight without danger in battles– Sun Tzu sixth century BC." She ran her fingers over the words, 'know your enemies'.

She closed the book and stared at the demon on the cover. He was different to the one she'd faced. No wings for starters. This one had short horns coming from his shoulder and upper arm, five on each side that became progressively smaller as they went down the arm. They looked more like talons than horns so she wasn't sure what to call them.

Opening the book again, she turned more pages, stopping at the contents. She frowned at the titles of some of the chapters. Holy Objects, Dangers of Unfulfilled Promises, Weapons and Uses, Temptation, Demon Hierarchy, Binding and Banishing Demons. Her gaze was drawn back to 'Weapons and Uses'. Now that chapter sounded helpful, the rest, not so much.

"My great-great grandfather wrote it." Alex entered with a bowl of soup and a glass of water on a tray. He placed it on the coffee table. "Gran asked if she could see you once you've eaten." Alex sat across from her. "She's actually my great-grandmother." He fell silent a moment. "Aren't you going to eat? It won't taste as good if you let it go cold."

"I'm not much for soup."

"At least have a couple of mouthfuls. Gran said it'd be the best thing for your stomach after not eating much recently."

Alyssa reluctantly put the book beside her and pulled the tray onto her lap. She hesitantly had a mouthful of soup. "It actually tastes okay."

"You don't have to sound so surprised. Although I'm sure a big part of it is hunger." Alex smiled slightly.

"Does it bother you?" Alyssa asked between mouthfuls.

"What?"

"Having to be a demon hunter?"

"You're wrong. No one'd force that decision on any of us. We're actually discouraged."

"Do you all end up hunters anyway?"

Alex shook his head. "Riley's brother, Blake, isn't one anymore."

"What happened?"

There was silence, then Alex spoke, "He decided it wasn't for him."

"And you can do that? Just decide not to do it anymore?"

"Yes. We have free will."

"Why did Riley ask me if I believe in God?"

"Where do demons reside?"

She swallowed her mouthful of soup before she answered. "Hell, I guess."

"And the opposite of hell?"

"Heaven. So you're saying that because they're opposites they can be used against each other?"

"Not quite. More along the lines of calling on the power of heaven to help fight the powers of hell."

"Does that mean I wouldn't have been able to win against the demon?"

"It means we must never leave you alone after dark and try and have you in a holy place by then."

"It… he's coming back? The demon. Not just Nathan, but both of them?"

Chapter Ten

Alex stared at her for a moment before he nodded. "Yes. Some demons can't handle the day. You were lucky in some ways he isn't a minor demon as most of them aren't bothered by the sun rising."

"How do we get rid of him?"

"That's something we have to figure out."

"What do you mean? He's a demon. Aren't you demon hunters?"

"If only it was that simple. Scarlett already tried to banish him. No two demons are the same. I guess you could say they're all a different sin. They're called by various methods and they're all asked to do something different for each person who summons them. We need to know everything you can recall about the summoning. And anything else Nathan might have said that can help us. Do you mind if I bring Gran in here to listen. She's been fighting demons her entire life."

"You said she's your great-grandmother." At Alex's nod, Alyssa asked, "Then how old does that make her?"

Alex laughed. "Relatively young if you ask her. She swears she's a long way off one hundred. We all tell her it's a sin to lie and she says time is in the eye of the one experiencing it."

"So she's nearly a hundred?" Alyssa's eyes widened.

Alex shrugged. "She's not saying. And anyone who knows for certain won't tell those of us who don't. You mind if I get her now?"

"I guess not."

Alex took the tray from her as he left the room and Alyssa turned back to the book. She opened to the first page and began to read, determined to know her enemy. She hadn't got far into the book before Alex returned. With him was his gran.

Alyssa's gaze was drawn to the elderly woman's left arm and was unable to move from there. The demon mark wound all the way up to nearly her shoulder. The same thin line evenly spaced, even with the wrinkles and skin that sagged in places. It took effort, but she finally managed to drag her gaze away to meet the hazel stare of the old woman. Her grey hair was pulled back from her lined face and plaited. She wore a cross on a thin gold chain and seemed both the oldest woman Alyssa had ever seen as well as completely ageless. Alyssa rose belatedly to her feet, clutching the book in her hands.

"So child, who are you?" The voice was surprisingly strong.

"Alyssa Evans."

"Do you prefer Alyssa or Allie, child?"

Alyssa shrugged.

"Good. Alyssa is too pretty a name to shorten." She sent a thin-lipped look towards Alex who shrugged. She turned back to Alyssa. "Call me Gran. Sit down, child. You look like a strong breeze would blow you over."

And you look like you could stand against a cyclone. Alyssa wished she had the courage to voice her thought.

Gran sat down and waved Alex to a seat, her gaze on Alyssa. "Now, start at the beginning and tell me everything."

Alyssa's cheeks grew hot and she sent a quick glance towards Alex.

"Never you mind him. He's done his share of stupid things," Gran said.

Alyssa looked towards Alex again. He winked at

her and his mouth curved into a fleeting smile. She quickly looked away, her gaze going to her hands that gripped the book. Surely they didn't expect her to start with the argument she had with her parents and hopping in Nathan's car. She glanced up at Gran. She sighed. She guessed they did.

Alyssa started hesitantly with frequent glances at Alex to see how he reacted. But he didn't. When neither Gran nor Alex interrupted with questions, she grew more confident. The only reaction she noticed Alex have was one of his fleeting smiles when she spoke of telling Nathan she'd come back and haunt him. When she reached the end, she fell silent. And waited. She looked down at the book in her hands. And continued to wait. She looked at Alex who leaned back in the armchair he sat in and quietly watched her. Her gaze was then drawn to Gran, who nodded thoughtfully.

Alyssa wanted to demand Gran tell her what she thought. She wanted to shake Alex and ask how he could be so relaxed when the daylight hours were rapidly disappearing. A demon waited for her. She gripped the book tighter.

Gran rose to her feet. "Have a sleep while you can, child. It'll be a long night."

When Gran turned to walk from the room, Alyssa

leapt to her feet. "That's it? That's all you can say? There's a bloody demon out there waiting for me, and you tell me to sleep. Forget it. I'd be better off on my own." She strode from the room, the book clutched to her chest. She perched on the edge of the shoebox and pulled on her boots and zipped them. "What do you want?" She eyed Alex warily.

"Anger isn't helpful."

"And you're so perfect you never have to deal with pesky human emotions like anger."

Alex smiled and his solemn expression changed dramatically. He held out his hand. "Come for a walk."

"What?"

Alex slid his feet into worn sneakers and opened the front door. He let his hand drop. "Come on."

"You're mad." Alyssa shook her head. "I'm out of here. Don't follow me." She tugged on the strap of her bag so it sat on her hip, strode out the door and glared at Alex as he fell in beside her.

"How did Nathan react when you told him you were going to come back and haunt him?"

"I don't understand you."

"I'm curious. You never said."

Alyssa stopped at the end of the driveway and turned to face Alex. One hand was on her hip and the other clutched the book to her chest. "I spill all my stupidity to you and all you're interested in is the reaction of that psychopath?"

"No. But it'll give me some sort of an indication of how far he's fallen."

"It bothered him. He urged me to give my soul to the demon so I couldn't haunt him. So what does that tell you, oh wise one?"

"You really do have a problem with anger management, don't you?"

"You didn't answer my question, Sir Perfect."

Alex chuckled. He reached out and drew the crimson lock of hair forward. His expression became serious again. "There was a lot of power floating around that clearing. Blood sacrifice, a demon, a soul, anger and an oath. He had reason to be scared. Don't trap your soul like that Alyssa. It isn't worth the revenge."

Alyssa pulled her hair from his fingers. "I'm not going to sit back and let him give me to his demon."

"It's not his demon. People forget that. He has no control over the demon that it doesn't let him have. Not a demon of that power. But even a minor demon can twist the terms to suit themselves. The saying 'be careful what you wish for' is very true when it comes to dealing with demons."

"And what am I meant to do? Sleep? Isn't that what your gran expects?"

"Gran's accustomed to people listening to her and doing as she says. She's the head of our family. The oldest one living. She'll consult with her children, her nieces and nephews, and their children. She doesn't know how to deal with this demon. Not ethically, anyway."

"Ethically?"

"We won't give him another living sacrifice in exchange for you. We won't use any other dark art to deal with him. We aren't perfect, Alyssa. All of us are human and sin at times. But we'd never commit a sin of such magnitude. We'll do all we possibly can to protect you. Sometimes all we'll be able to do is stand between you and the demon. I'm sorry about that. But we only have to keep you safe for a month before the demon'll turn on those who've called him to pay their debt. Not ideal, but at least it should be some comfort to you."

"So what's that mean? I live in a church for the next month?"

"Not quite." Alex smiled fleetingly. "But you'll find nights to be lacking in sleep. That's why Gran suggested you sleep now. Will you come back to our home? Have some sleep? It'll be a long night."

"And what about you? When will you sleep? Didn't you say you'd stand between me and the demon?"

"Riley will watch over you in an hour. Then it'll be my turn to sleep."

Alyssa shook her head. "He's too-" she searched for the right word.

"It's his way of coping. You've seen what we face. His way of dealing with it is the jokes and smiles. You can trust him with your life."

"That's what you're expecting me to do."

"I know. And you don't know us, but I swear we'll put ourselves between you and the demon."

"Even though I brought it on myself."

"Oh, no, don't think that." Alex reached out and wrapped his arms around her. She held herself rigid for a second before she melted against him. "No one deserves this. The blame lies squarely on Nathan and Brian's shoulders. You didn't do anything to deserve this. Come on, let's go back inside." He drew back slightly to look down at her. "Sleep?"

Alyssa sighed and pulled back reluctantly from the warmth of Alex's arms. "Sure. Sleep. Why not?"

Alex took her free hand and walked to the front door with her. "You'll feel a little better after a sleep."

"I slept for ages while I was... when..."

"Not the same. You'll be able to relax and sleep without fear. I'll watch over you."

Alyssa smiled wryly. "What? You going to be my guardian angel?"

"If that's what it takes."

"Don't you have to be dead to be an angel? Or in heaven? But then you've got to be dead to be in heaven." Alyssa frowned.

They paused in the doorway of the bedroom Alyssa had dressed in earlier. Alex met her gaze. "Whatever it takes, Alyssa. We're sworn to protect the innocent from demons. And I personally swore I'd stand between you and the demon."

"But-"

Alex shook his head, "Sleep now. Argue later."

"I wasn't going to argue. And don't smile at me like that." She strode in and sat on the edge of the bed. As soon as her boots were unzipped, she dropped them on the carpet. She looked towards Alex who had kicked off his sneakers and now sat on the duchess, one knee drawn up for his chin to rest on. "You won't leave me alone?"

Alex shook his head. "Sleep. One of us'll be with you the entire time. I promise."

Alyssa hesitated. She didn't know Alex, but his words made her feel safe. She pulled back the bed linen, dropped her handbag on the floor and climbed in between the sheets, holding the book. As she closed her eyes, her last sight was of Alex sitting on the duchess, watching over her. Her last thought was of the three demon hunters with their swords drawn as they faced the demon. She didn't want any of them to die in her stead.

Chapter Eleven

The smell of freshly cooked meat teased her nose. Her mouth began to water. She rolled over and opened her eyes. Scarlett sat not far from the bed, a tray in front of her with steak and vegetables piled on a plate. With her mouth full, Scarlett pointed to the bedside cabinet with her fork. Alyssa glanced over and saw a tray with the same meal as well as a glass of water, cutlery and a serviette.

"Thank you," Alyssa said huskily as she sat up and reached for the tray. She had a long drink first. Then she cut off some meat and filled her fork with it and vegetables. It quickly went in her mouth. She caught Scarlett's frown before it cleared. "What?" Alyssa asked when she'd swallowed her food.

Scarlett shook her head.

"You were frowning at me."

"Have you ever been to Mass?"

"Huh?"

"It's Sunday, Allie. The church we'll be going to has Mass Sunday evening. We'll be arriving just before it starts."

"Isn't there somewhere else we can go?"

"No."

"Is that what made you frown?"

Scarlett shook her head. "Not exactly. You didn't say grace."

"I… what?"

"Thank you God for the food I am about to eat."

"Oh."

"I didn't expect you to. It just made me wonder how you'll cope sitting through the entire Mass."

"What do I have to do?"

"Follow what the rest of us do. Except when we…. ahh… do you know any religious terms?"

"Just what I've seen in movies. I'm guessing you're about to say when you go up for the wafer thing and wine."

Scarlett winced and slowly shook her head. "Yes, I was. I'll let you know when you have to stay in the pew. Seat," she quickly amended when Alyssa frowned.

"Why didn't you just say seat to start with?"

There was a light tap on the door, before it opened

slowly. Alex stood in the doorway. He glanced first at Scarlett sitting on the floor before his gaze came to rest on Alyssa. He remained in the doorway.

"When you've finished your meal, I'll be in the lounge room. Can you join me there?"

"What for?" Alyssa's eyes narrowed. "What's wrong?"

Alex shook his head. "Everything's exactly the same. I just want to go over a few things with you."

"Are you sure?"

"We don't lie," Scarlett said.

"It's okay, Scarlett. She doesn't know us. Trust takes time to build." Alex looked back at Alyssa. "No need to rush."

Alyssa watched as Alex closed the door then looked down at Scarlett. "Do you know what that was about?"

Scarlett shrugged. "It could be anything. There's so much you don't know." Scarlett held her hand up when Alyssa opened her mouth, leaning forward as she did so. "Don't take it personally. It's a statement, nothing more."

Alyssa closed her mouth and looked at her food. She stabbed a piece of meat with her fork. She was getting sick of being left in the dark. Of being the only one who didn't know exactly what was going on. She thought Alex telling her not to rush was a joke. Of course she'd rush.

As soon as she finished eating, Alyssa put the tray on the bedside cabinet. She threw back the sheets, slung her bag over one shoulder and grabbed the book with one hand, her boots with the other. She paused when she saw her boots were clean.

"Your clothes were washed and dried while you slept and your boots cleaned."

"Thanks." Alyssa strode to the door. "But I never want to see those clothes again." She opened the door and headed for the lounge room. As she walked past the two shoeboxes, she dropped her boots in front of one of them.

Alex rose from the armchair he sat in when she entered the room. He held a paperback book out to her. She moved forward and took it. She glanced from it to the hardback book she held in her other hand.

"A paperback version. You can keep it. We've had them reprinted. They make a good textbook."

Alyssa handed back the one she'd carried around all afternoon. "I need to know what I can do. I can't sit around and expect you to protect me. I need to be able to protect myself." Alyssa frowned as Alex pulled a laminated card from his pocket and handed it to her.

"Learn this then."

"The Lord's Prayer? You've got to be kidding me. You all carry around swords and I'm armed with a prayer?"

"Have you used a sword before?"

Alyssa shook her head. "How hard can it be?"

"Then you're safer with the prayer."

"I want a sword."

"The swords work because they've been blessed and we believe in the blessing. This is the prayer Jesus taught and it's found in the bible. The demon will fear this prayer on your lips far more than he'll fear a blessed sword in your hands."

"That's ridiculous."

"Whether you find it ridiculous or not, it's the truth. If you really want to help yourself, you'll learn that prayer. You don't need to believe a single word for it to work. History's done that job for you. And here." He held out a cross on a leather necklace.

"I don't believe in that."

"Take it and wear it. And think on it. Without night, there'd be no day. Without sorrow there'd be no joy. You've seen a demon with your own eyes."

Alyssa reluctantly took the necklace and put it on. "What about people that say religion brainwashes you?"

"People?"

Alyssa felt her cheeks heat. She muttered, "My parents."

"Free will, Alyssa. We're given free will so we can choose."

"But how do you know what you're believing is the truth? What if you can't take it on faith?"

"Then use logic. You'll be one of the few handfuls of people in the world who can. Or do you think the demon was a group hallucination? Those cuts on your arms weren't made for the fun of it. Nathan cut you for a purpose."

"Were you ever a child, Alex?"

"What?"

Alyssa smiled sadly. It was nice to see someone other than herself confused for a change. Even if it was only for a second. "You're so serious all the time. I'd swear you carry the weight of the world on your shoulders. Were you always serious? Were you ever a child? Did you laugh and play? Or were you only ever focused on standing between the world and demons?"

"Childhood can be a fleeting dream."

"What's that supposed to mean?"

Alex shook his head. "How attached are you to that handbag? A backpack'd be more sensible."

Alyssa sighed. Even more unanswered questions. She recognised a brick wall when she saw one. "I can use a backpack." She was surprised when he moved to the armchair he'd been sitting on and picked up a backpack from the floor. "What's in it?" Alyssa asked as she took it.

"Simple first aid kit, shallow bowl, cup, cutlery, food, water, change of clothes, money, notebook with emergency contact details, thermal blanket, salt and holy water."

"Salt! That must have been what Brian sprinkled to make the circle. Isn't that black magic?"

"If for some reason you're separated from us, make a circle with the salt, sprinkle the holy water on it and start reciting the Lord's Prayer. And don't step out of the circle no matter what happens."

"Are we likely to be separated?" Fear rushed through her and threatened to swamp her. "You said you'd stand between me and the demon."

"If it's at all humanly possible I'll be there between you and the demon. The salt is a precaution."

"Humanly possible? What are you trying to say? Enough with the riddles. Spell it out in plain English."

Alex watched her carefully before he nodded. "If I die defending you I want you to know another way to protect yourself."

"No." Alyssa swallowed with difficulty and shook her head vehemently. "You're not to die."

"Alyssa-"

"No!"

"You asked for plain speaking."

"Fine. And I'm telling you it won't happen. None of you are to die for me. Do you hear me? I got myself into this fix. I won't have anyone die because of my stupidity. Not Erin, not my parents and not you or Scarlett or Riley."

"I swore I'd stand between you and the demon. To me that's a binding agreement."

"No!"

"Death is always a possibility, but I'll do my best to-"

"You'll do better than that. I couldn't live with the death of one of you on my conscience."

"We won't talk about it anymore," Alex said softly.

"We won't talk about it because it isn't going to happen." Alyssa glared at him.

"What won't happen?" Riley asked from the doorway.

Alyssa turned to see Riley and Scarlett in the doorway, black clothes, swords slung across their backs and backpacks on one shoulder. Riley held Alex's sword. He strode forward and took it.

"None of you are to die for me. I won't have it. If it is between you or me, let him have me," Alyssa stated.

"Aww, sweetheart, I didn't know you cared for us so much." Riley grinned. "Want to catch a movie once this is all over?"

"Be serious," Alyssa snapped.

Riley's expression became solemn. "I'm hurt. How could you think I wasn't serious?"

"Give it up, Riley. She's got your number." Scarlett elbowed Riley in the ribs.

"Unappreciated. Unloved. Might as well go out to the car." Riley turned to go.

"Passenger seat," Alex said.

"Control freak." Riley grinned before he hurried away.

"Are you two ready?" Scarlett asked.

"I think Alyssa needs a few minutes to get what she needs out of her handbag and put it in the backpack," Alex said.

Alyssa nodded. She crouched on the floor and dumped out the contents of her handbag. "I won't be long." She grabbed what she thought she might need, including her phone, makeup and brush, and shoved it in the backpack. The rest she pushed in her bag. "Is there somewhere I can leave this until it's all over?" She held up her handbag as she rose to her feet.

Scarlett took it from her. "I'll put it in my wardrobe for you." She frowned. "Actually, I'll get someone to wash it in saltwater first. It's been marked with your blood."

"Why saltwater and is the blood a problem?"

"The saltwater will neutralise the blood which is what he'll use to track you," Scarlet said.

"Oh." Alyssa stared at the dark marks on her bag.

"Problem?" Alex asked.

"I don't know. The baby wipes I used to clean the blood off my face, I threw them in a bin at the elevator." Alyssa was alarmed by the look Alex and Scarlett shared. "What? What's wrong?"

"Let's get you to the church before dark." Alex placed his hand on the small of her back.

Alyssa pulled away. "What's wrong?"

"Not wrong exactly. It just would've been a better idea if we could've disposed of them properly," Alex said.

"There's the side benefit it might slow him down," Scarlett said.

Alex shook his head. "No. Wrong direction. By now they'll be at the rubbish tip. She'll be the first blood he'll find in the direction he's coming from."

"How do you know where he'll come from?" Alyssa asked.

"He'll appear in the place he disappeared."

Scarlett held Alyssa's bag up. "I'll get this taken care of and meet you at the car."

Alex waited until Scarlett left the room before he turned to Alyssa. "Are you ready to go?"

"I don't suppose you have a spare toothbrush so I can clean my teeth before we leave?" Alyssa asked wistfully.

"Bathroom. Vanity cupboard."

"Thanks." Alyssa headed to the bathroom and paused in the doorway. It was spotless. The towel she'd used earlier was gone, her pile of clothes on the floor also missing. No trace of her. Like she'd never been in here. Alyssa forced herself to take a step forward. They wouldn't remove her from life so easily.

"Alyssa."

She turned to face Alex who'd come to stand in the doorway.

"I didn't think to pack a toothbrush for you in the backpack. There are travel cases in the cupboard you can put the toothbrush in when you're finished. Toothpaste too."

As soon as Alyssa nodded, Alex moved away from the doorway. She quickly found an unopened toothbrush, travel case and toothpaste. As soon as she'd finished in the bathroom and packed the items in her backpack she walked into the entrance hall. Alex stood by the front door, his back to her. She hurried to the shoebox and sat on the edge as she pulled on her boots. At the sound of the zip being pulled up, Alex turned towards her.

"What?" Alyssa asked when Alex continued to watch her silently.

He shook his head. "Never mind. Let's go."

Alyssa walked over to stand in front of him. "What were you going to say?"

Alex smiled wryly. "It seems even I have my limit on the questions I'm willing to ask. Come on. We have to get to our church before it's dark."

If Alyssa had something, she'd have thrown it at the back of Alex's head. Instead, she stalked after him as he walked towards the car. She was nearly there when she stopped suddenly. It was a different car. A sleek, dark coloured car with the words 'all wheel drive' written on the side.

"Come on, Allie." Riley swung the back door open and slid across the seat to make room for her.

She ignored Riley, strode after Alex and grabbed hold of his arm. "What did you mean back there?"

"Nothing, Alyssa. Forget it."

"No."

"Get in the car. Before I put you in there."

"You–"

"This isn't a game. We need to be at the church before Mass starts. We can't walk in there with our swords when people start arriving. They need to be stashed before then. Now get in the car. It's going to be a long night. I'm sure you'll have more than enough time to give me the third degree."

Alyssa's lips thinned. "Fine." She pulled the car door open and glared at Riley who moved across the back seat and pulled the other door shut. She slammed her door and stared out the window. She sat silent throughout the drive. Her gaze focused on the window, even though most of what she saw was little more than a blur. What she did see, and far too clearly, was the demon. It didn't matter if her eyes were open or closed.

Chapter Twelve

When the car eventually came to a stop, Alyssa blinked and glanced around to get her bearings. Alex opened her door and waited patiently for her to climb out. Alyssa hopped out in time to see Scarlett put the swords into a rectangular case with a handle, and latched it shut. Riley took the case from her and strode to the church. Alyssa silently followed him and Scarlett, Alex at her side.

She watched as they dipped their fingers into the bowl of water just inside the church and touch their forehead, chest and both shoulders. She glanced questioningly towards Alex who shook his head. Relieved, she entered the church and looked around. This was the first time she'd been in a church. To her it seemed full of shadows and dark timber. The stained glass did little to brighten things. Her gaze shied away from the cross behind the altar and she watched as both Scarlett and Riley half knelt, crossed themselves again and sat in the last pew. Riley put the case with the swords under their seat.

Alyssa glanced to Alex who looked like he was about to smile. "What?" Her word came out as a whisper. Anything louder would have seemed out of place.

Alex shook his head, gesturing towards where Riley and Scarlett sat. "Take a seat, Alyssa. No need to pay respect for what you don't believe in. But I will ask you to kneel when everyone else does during Mass. It's the least you can do for the sanctuary you've accepted."

Unable to meet his gaze, Alyssa looked at the ground. She hurried to the pew, sat beside Riley and dropped her backpack near her feet like she'd seen Riley and Scarlett do. Alex did the same half kneel and crossed himself before he entered the pew to sit on her left. He was barely seated when he slid forward to kneel on the wooden board that ran the length of the pew. He rested his arms on the pew in front, and bowed his head. Alyssa glanced at Riley and Scarlett who continued to remain seated.

She sat there quietly, with nothing to distract her when she desperately needed something to take her mind off the rapidly approaching night. The hard timber of the pew made her shift as she tried to get more comfortable. She glanced towards Alex who still knelt in prayer. She turned to Riley and Scarlett on her other side and then frowned. Frowning, she looked back to Alex and then Riley and Scarlett again.

"Riley. It's nearly summer."

"So?"

"You're all wearing long sleeve shirts. Aren't you melting?"

Riley shrugged.

"That isn't an answer."

Scarlett leaned in front of Riley. "Of course we're hot, Allie. That should be obvious to anyone."

Alyssa took a deep breath and pushed away the angry retort that came to her lips. She turned back to Riley. "Why?"

Riley grinned. "Why are we hot? Because we're wearing long sleeve shirts in late spring."

"Riley." Alyssa said his name through clenched teeth. She nearly jumped as Alex tugged on her arm to get her attention.

"Do you mind?" Alex's gaze travelled from Alyssa to Riley. "You should know better." He looked at Alyssa again. "People get the wrong idea about the demon marks when we go out as a group. They usually think it's a gang tattoo." He turned away and bowed his head in prayer again.

Alyssa stared straight ahead and tried to ignore the heat in her cheeks.

Riley leaned near and bent his head close to her ear. "Sorry." He shifted away again.

Alyssa ignored him. A sound in the direction of the altar made Alyssa look over as her heart rate sped up. She sagged slightly when she saw it was a priest. She watched him walk down the aisle. As he drew close, Alex crossed himself and sat back in the pew. The priest stopped with a smile of welcome.

Alyssa was surprised at how young he looked. She guessed he was about thirty. When she noticed how good-looking he was, she had the fleeting thought of, what a waste. She glanced apologetically towards the cross at the front of the church.

"Father Joe." Alex said.

"How are you, Alex?" Father Joe looked towards the rest of them. "And you Scarlett and Riley." He smiled at Alyssa. "Nice to see a new face in my church."

They all murmured greetings except Alyssa, who quickly looked away. She felt like she was there under false pretences.

"Do you have a minute, Father?" Alex rose to his feet. "For confession?"

"How many sins could you have committed in three days, Alex? My congregation will start arriving in about five minutes. Are you sure your sins can't be absolved during Mass?"

"It won't take long, Father."

Father Joe's smile evaporated. He shifted enough to be able to look under the pew. He looked first at Alyssa and then at Riley and Scarlett. "And you two?"

"Just your blessing, Father," Riley said.

"Always," Father Joe said solemnly. "Come on then, Alex."

As soon as the two had moved away, Alyssa turned to Riley. "What was that all about?"

"I don't think we have time for Religion 101."

"How about you give me the highlights then?" Alyssa glared at Riley.

"You can be so dense at times, Alyssa," Scarlett said.

Alyssa's mouth opened. She stared at Scarlett who sat back so Riley blocked Alyssa's view of her.

Riley took Alyssa's hand and patted it. "Mass will start shortly. There's no time for this discussion."

Alyssa tugged her hand out of his grasp. "But you won't tell me later, will you? You all tell me as little as possible."

"You have a tendency to freak when we tell you too much," Riley said.

Angry words rose to her lips. She even opened her mouth to speak them. Then she recalled where she was. She reached down to her backpack and pulled out the book by Patrick Hunter and opened it. She ignored the quiet chuckle from Riley and barely glanced up when Alex returned to sit beside her. She became so immersed in the book she was startled to see how many people filled the church when Alex tugged on her elbow to make her rise like the rest of the congregation.

The sounds of an organ filled the church and all around her people began to sing. Some held books they sang from, others had no need, for they obviously knew the songs well. Alyssa glanced at the demon hunters, their hands clasped before them, eyes forward as they sang.

Typical, Alyssa thought in annoyance. Someone should make them saints. She looked around and wished she could go back to her book. She needed to learn as much as possible about demons and Patrick had a way with words that made him able to impart information without the reader's eyes glazing in boredom.

Alyssa's mouth dropped open as her gaze drifted

over the congregation. In the last pew, across the aisle from them, stood Nathan. When Alyssa tried to run, Alex grabbed her by one arm, Riley by the other.

"Nathan," Alyssa hissed and tried to pull her arms from their grips.

"We're in a crowded church. You're safe for now." Alex tugged her down as everyone began to sit.

"We can't stay here."

"Don't make a scene."

Alyssa stared at Alex, surprised at the tone of his voice. "I-"

"Quiet. These people have come together to worship. Show some respect."

Alyssa glared at Alex before she faced forward. She seethed all through the Mass. She sent occasional glances towards Nathan and he caught her twice. Both times he winked at her. After the second time, she forced herself not to look at him again.

When the last hymn was sung and people started to leave the church, Alyssa tried to rise only to be pressed back in her seat by both Alex and Riley.

Alyssa leaned close to Alex. "Let go of me."

"You can't leave."

"Alex-"

"No. Trust me on this. Remember what I promised you?"

"Only to stand between me and the demon. Nathan's a man."

"Please, Alyssa. Don't fight us on this. We've been protecting people for years. We know what we're doing."

"You're the same age as me. How much experience could you have?"

"The first time I faced a demon I was ten."

Alyssa stared at him, speechless. She shook her head, trying to order her thoughts. "Is that… normal? I mean, normal in your family?"

Alex smiled fleetingly. "No." He rose abruptly and stepped out of the pew as Father Joe walked inside after seeing his parishioners off.

Father Joe looked between the five people left in the church. He walked towards Nathan. "Can I help you?"

Nathan's lips twisted into a humourless smile. "Not at all, Father. I need to talk to the kids."

"I'm afraid I need to lock up," Father Joe said.

"I'll just wait for the kids to head out then." Nathan glanced towards Alyssa.

"It's okay, Father Joe," Alex said.

"Are you sure?" Father Joe glanced towards Nathan who continued to lean back in the pew, an arm propped negligently along the backrest, a foot on the pew in front of him.

"As well as can be expected." Alex reached out to him with his left hand. Father Joe automatically did the same and they clasped hand to forearm so their wrists touched.

"May God watch over you," Father Joe said.

"Pray for us." Alex released Father Joe's arm.

Riley moved to stand near Alex. "The streets won't be safe tonight for those who see."

Scarlet pulled the case from under the pew and unlatched it. She took out her sword and slipped her arm and head through the strap so it hung on her back. She picked up the other two swords and stood next to Alex and Riley. "We'll be fine, Uncle Joe."

Alyssa's mouth dropped open with an audible sound. "How many of you are there?"

Father Joe chuckled. "We can be rather overwhelming all together. But I've filled the church with only family before. Usually for a baptism, wedding or funeral."

Alyssa glanced around the spacious interior of the church, unable to comprehend a family large enough to fill it. Or a family that kept in close contact with each other.

Nathan rose to his feet. "Family. That puts a

different slant on things. I don't think you should be going anywhere, Father."

Chapter Thirteen

"This is between us, Nathan. Father Joe has no part in it." Alex took his sword from Scarlett as Riley reached for his.

"Wrong. This is between Allie and myself. You're the one pushing yourself in where you don't belong."

Alex slung his sword on his back and continued to meet Nathan's gaze. "You're wrong. You called up a demon, that makes it our business."

Alyssa moved closer to Alex to stand behind him. She noticed Father Joe, Riley and Scarlett spread out a little. Nathan ignored them, pulling a gun from his jacket.

"And this says it's none of your business." Nathan waved with his gun towards the door. "Now get out of here and stay out of things that don't concern you."

"This is a house of God," Father Joe said.

Nathan laughed. "I'm sure he's seen guns before."

"Where's your father, Nathan? How come he's left you to do the dirty work for him?" Alex asked.

"He has a charity function he has to attend. He'd be missed if he didn't turn up. Nice try, but you won't get us to turn on each other."

"How did you find us?" Riley asked.

"Where else could you hide other than a church? I know the demon's level of power. It had to be an old church. You'd have been better off leaving the city if you hoped to keep me off your trail. Now quit stalling. I want Allie."

Scarlett moved closer to Nathan, coming in from his left. "Hell isn't a pleasant place. I hope you realise that's where you're headed."

"Back off, little girl. And keep your bible crap for someone else." Nathan turned the gun towards her.

It all happened in a split second. The moment the gun was off him, Alex launched himself at Nathan. Scarlett dropped to the ground as she saw the gun come her way and Riley attacked Nathan a moment after Alex. The gun skittered across the floor and Alyssa raced forward to grab it.

"Looks like you're a little outnumbered there, Nathan." Alyssa held the gun on him.

Alex was immediately on his feet. Riley was left to grapple with Nathan. Alex stood in front of Alyssa.

"Get out of the way, Alex." Alyssa held the gun steadily pointed straight ahead.

"Let it go, Alyssa," Alex said softly.

"No."

"We're in a church." Scarlett got to her feet.

"So? He started waving a gun at me first." Alyssa kept her gaze on Nathan who'd broken free of Riley and now backed away from him. Alyssa stepped sideways to have a clear view.

"Don't do this." Alex came to stand beside her. "Give me the gun."

"Get away from me, Alex."

"It's not in you to be able to kill him and live with yourself." Alex held out his hand.

"It's not in me to let him go after all he's put me through."

"Alyssa, is it?" Father Joe came to stand on her other side.

"Don't you start on me, Father. I don't believe in all this stuff." Alyssa gestured towards the altar with her left hand.

"We've got it under control, Father Joe," Riley said.

Father Joe looked steadily at each of them in turn. "Lock up when you're done." He began to walk towards the altar.

Alyssa started to laugh. She glanced at Alex, not

wanting to take her gaze off Nathan for more than a second. "Your family's insane."

Alex smiled fleetingly. "So we've been told before." He sighed. "Can I have the gun please, Alyssa?"

She shook her head. She glanced towards the altar and saw Father Joe disappear through a door she hadn't noticed in the shadows before. She looked around at the faces that watched her.

"Ask him why he's in here. I bet he hasn't stepped in a church for years, if ever," Alex said. "And I bet it isn't just because you're in here."

"Ask him what's out there waiting for him," Scarlett said. "He has no circle of power to protect him now. And his friend's waiting to be paid. I bet he's getting impatient after the taste he had when he was called."

"What's out there, Nathan?" Alyssa smiled, one as equally mirthless as many of Nathan's had been. "You have a friend waiting for you? I've just finished reading something about what happens to those who try and trick demons. I wonder what he thinks about not getting the sacrifice you promised him?"

"Oh it won't be me, Princess. You're the one who's going to go out there." Nathan pulled out another gun.

"Aw hell!" Riley groaned. "Who carts around two guns?"

"Riley!" Scarlett glared at him.

Riley glanced towards the altar and briefly closed his eyes. He then looked at Scarlett, an eyebrow raised momentarily.

Scarlett slowly shook her head in answer before she turned to face Nathan. "You can't shoot her. He want's a living sacrifice."

"Maiming will be just as painful," Nathan warned.

"How many of us do you think you'll be able to shoot before we reach you?" Alex stepped away from Alyssa.

"You better start deciding what you're going to do now before it's too late to do anything." Riley took a step towards Nathan.

"All of you freeze. She doesn't need to live." Nathan moved the gun so it was pointed at Scarlett.

"Same holds true for you, Nathan. I don't have to kill, just maim." Alyssa lowered the gun so it was pointed towards his legs.

"Have you ever used a gun before?" Nathan asked.

"Guess we'll soon find out if you don't put your gun down." Alyssa grinned. "Don't put the gun down, Nathan. I really, really want to pull this trigger."

"Please, Alyssa." Alex moved closer to his sister. "Don't shed his blood in a church."

"Well I don't think he's about to step outside so I can shoot him."

Nathan laughed. "Still making jokes I see. You're on the wrong team, Princess. You'd have done much better by my side."

"I'm giving you till the count of five. And we never would have suited. I don't hang out with scum."

"You could have fooled me." Nathan glanced briefly towards Riley. "Don't move boy. Your friend here won't last long if you don't stay still."

"One."

"I don't believe you've ever held a gun in your life." Nathan took a step forward. "Come on, Princess. I dare you."

Alyssa took a step towards Nathan. "Two… three."

Nathan looked towards Riley again, his gun moved to aim at him instead. "I don't like to repeat myself."

Alex launched himself at the same time Riley dropped to the ground. The gun fired and the sound echoed in the church. Alyssa ran forward and stomped on Nathan's hand that Alex pressed against the floor. As soon as he let go of the gun she kicked it towards Riley who picked himself up off the floor.

"Throw him outside," Alyssa snarled.

"No." Riley put the safety on before he tucked the gun into the back of his jeans. He waved Scarlett away who'd run to his side to check he was alive. "We won't have a hand in his death."

"Are you lot mad? He'd do that to us." Alyssa swore as she stared at each of them in turn. "He'd do worse."

"It's not our job to punish him," Scarlett said softly. "I know he tried to kill you. I know you think right now you want to do the same to him. But it'd start to eat at you if you did. Maybe not right away. Maybe a week from now, maybe a year, but it'd happen."

Alyssa shook her head. "No. It wouldn't."

"Well, why don't you see, Princess? You're holding a gun. Show me if you have the guts."

"Get away from him, Alex. Let's see if he's still smiling after I shoot him." Alyssa kept the gun pointed steadily at Nathan.

Alex shook his head. He sat on Nathan's back, one of Nathan's arms twisted high behind him. "You don't really mean it, Alyssa. Once you calm down you'll feel different." He glanced behind her.

Alyssa turned to see what Alex looked at. She saw Scarlett rummaging in her backpack. "What's going on?" She looked between Alex, Riley and Scarlett.

Scarlett strode towards Nathan, two lengths of rope in her hands. "We can't let him wander free. Who knows what other weapons he has stashed on himself."

"No! You have to send him to the demon. Do you think he's going to let me live? I want to go home. End it!"

Alex swiftly tied Nathan's hands behind his back and then used the other piece to wrap his ankles tightly together. He strode towards Alyssa the moment his task was complete. "Give me the gun."

"No. It's mine."

"Then at least put the safety on so you don't accidentally shoot yourself."

"I don't know how."

"Give it here and I'll do it for you." Alex held out his hand.

"I wasn't born yesterday, Alex."

Alex sighed heavily. "I promise to give it back to you."

Alyssa hesitated.

"Oh for crying out loud," Scarlett said. "How many times have I got to tell you we don't lie? I can't watch any more of this drama. If you need me I'll be as far away from all this rot as I can get without leaving the church." Scarlett strode towards the pew where they'd left their backpacks. She grabbed hers and headed for the front of the church.

Alex continued to hold out his hand. "Alyssa?"

Alyssa glanced between Scarlett's retreating back and Alex. She reluctantly handed the gun to him and watched as he put the safety on, taking the gun when he held it out. She tucked it into the back of her jeans and tried to shift it to a more comfortable position, with no luck. Resigned to the discomfit, she moved to where Riley checked Nathan for weapons. He found a pocketknife and ammunition. Alyssa grabbed the ammunition.

"Allie-" Riley began, but stopped immediately at the look she sent him. He shrugged and glanced towards Alex who nodded. Riley grabbed his backpack and walked towards Scarlett.

"You certainly know how to clear a room, Princess."

"Shut up."

"You wound me." Nathan smirked.

Alyssa turned away from Nathan. Alex watched her. She turned away from him too. She grabbed her backpack and moved to the back of the church. She pulled out the thin blanket and rolled it up as a pillow and lay on her side to read her book.

It wasn't fair. High school was over. Forever. She could sleep to eight every day since it didn't take her long to get to work. That meant she'd have had plenty of time to catch a movie with Erin tonight. They could have stopped in at Del's first. Or even gone there after the movie so they could argue over which was the best scene. Instead she was stuck in a church with a demon prowling around outside waiting for her. She was living the horror movie.

Her eyes blinked rapidly as she tried to focus on the words of the book. She couldn't think about what waited for her. She had to figure out how to deal with it. The words came into focus. Her enemy better look out because she was getting to know him better with each page.

Chapter Fourteen

"Alyssa."

She opened her eyes. Her heart raced at the sound of her name whispered. Looking up she saw Alex crouched beside her. She took a shuddering breath and closed her eyes for a second. When she opened them, she felt a little more in control. Sitting up, she stretched. She frowned when she saw Riley and Scarlett by the church door, their backpacks on, the sword case in Riley's hand.

"Time to go." Alex pressed his fingers to her lips when she opened her mouth to speak. "Shh." He nodded towards where Nathan lay on his side, his eyes closed, his knife beside him.

Alyssa packed up her gear and followed Alex outside to where Riley and Scarlett hurried to the car. As soon as they were far enough from the church, Alyssa asked, "Where are we going now?"

"Up the coast. Blake has an apartment only a few hours from here. We'll sleep there for a bit and figure out where to go next. We can't stay around here."

Alyssa stopped in mid stride as her hand touched the small of her back. "Where is it? What've you done with my gun?"

"In your backpack."

Alyssa slipped her hand inside and ignored the hurt expression on Alex's face. She felt relieved when she found the cold metal. "Sorry."

"Forget it." Alex looked away, his expression closed again.

"I have to work today."

"Find someone to replace you."

"Just like that? You think people will drop what they're doing and take over my job for me and then return it when this is over?"

"I'm not fighting with you. If you don't know someone who can take over, ring and quit. You can't go to work if you want to live."

Alyssa hurried ahead of Alex. She fumbled in her backpack for her phone. As soon as she was in the car, she dialled Erin.

"Sleeping," Erin mumbled.

"Can you do me a favour?"

"What? Allie? Where are you? What are you doing

ringing at this hour? Don't you know what time it is?"

"I changed my mind about Cairns. But I'm a long way from home. Do you think you can fill in for me at work until I get back? Might take me a couple of weeks. I know you're working weekends, but you did say you wished you could get more hours."

"Where are you? What happened to Cairns?"

"Erin! Focus."

"Sure. I'll save your butt. Again. You owe me though."

"You have no idea."

"Then how about you tell me so I have one."

"I can't right now. Look, I've got to go. I need to keep some credit on my phone."

"Call your parents, Allie. They're driving me nuts. And they've got my parents on my back."

"Sorry. I just don't know what to say to them."

"Yeah well, think of something. And tell them to quit ringing me."

"Sorry, Erin. When I get more credit on my phone I'll call my parents and talk to them."

"Promise?"

"Sure. I promise."

"Okay. Hey, you'll never believe who I thought I saw yesterday."

Alyssa hoped Erin wasn't going to make it a guessing game. "Who?"

"Nathan. I mean, I didn't get that good a look at him, but I swear it was him."

Alyssa's heart seemed to stop and she closed her eyes as she tried to hold back the fear that threatened to swamp her. "You sure?"

"Nope, not really. Why?"

What could she say without having to explain far too much and panic Erin? "It wasn't important."

"Okay. You going to tell me anything of what's been happening?"

"No."

"Then I'm going back to sleep. No human should be awake at this hour. I'd throw something at you if you were here."

"Bye, Erin."

"Mmmm."

Alyssa turned to Riley. "Erin saw Nathan."

"It doesn't matter. We've got people watching over her." Riley grinned momentarily. "Her own guardian angels."

Alyssa couldn't return his grin. "She'll be okay? And my parents?"

"Yes. And speaking of your parents." Riley gave her a card. "Call your parents. Didn't you promise your friend you'd call when you had more credit for your phone."

"That's cheating."

Riley grinned. "So? Give them a call. They must be out of their mind with worry."

Alyssa reluctantly took the card. "We're not close like your family."

"They deserve a call."

"They'll yell at me and carry on."

Riley shrugged. "That's their problem. Not yours. No need to take it on board."

"What do you think you are? My shrink?" Alyssa glanced towards Scarlett who laughed. "He's not, is he?"

"Not yet. He's still at uni," Scarlett said.

"You don't think I spend all my time fighting demons, do you?"

Alyssa stared at Riley in disbelief. "But a shrink?"

Riley shrugged. "I find people fascinating. Now quit stalling. Call your parents."

"It's too early. They'll be asleep," Alyssa protested.

"That might be the best time to ring them. Catch them off guard."

"I don't know, Riley."

Riley shrugged again. "Might not be as inclined to yell at you."

Alyssa stared at the card. "I'll ring them after breakfast."

"Guess our next stop is a servo with a restaurant. And we'll need fuel before we get to Blake's," Alex said.

Alyssa glared at him. The last thing she wanted to do was ring her parents. Her days were bad enough without the extra trauma.

* * *

Alyssa wished she'd rung her parents while they were at the service station. She'd been so busy putting the chore off she'd forgotten she'd have an audience in the car. Scarlet was on her small laptop, Alex drove as usual and Riley read a magazine he'd bought during their stop. A financial magazine. It was the last sort of magazine she'd expected him to buy, let alone read.

She stared at her phone. She'd left it on after ringing Erin and not once had her mother tried to ring. She looked at how much charge was left on her phone and smiled. If she was lucky, she wouldn't be able to talk long before the battery went flat.

She dialled her home number and waited for someone to answer.

"Hello?"

"Mum."

Silence stretched out, before Grace spoke again. "Come home, Alyssa."

"I'm sorry, Mum."

"Running from problems doesn't solve them."

"I know. But not being listened to doesn't help either."

"Is that what all this is about?"

"Not exactly."

"Then what is it?"

"I didn't want to have to walk out like that. But I'm not a child. I know I have to live by your rules while I'm in your home, so maybe that's the solution."

"What are you trying to say?"

"That living at home might not be the best option for me."

"Don't be ridiculous, Alyssa. You can't afford to move out of home. Not and go to uni as well."

"Then maybe that's the rest of the solution."

"You're going to uni, and that's final."

"See, that's the problem, Mum. No discussion. You tell me to do something and I'm expected to immediately jump to it. I'm not a child."

"You're our child. Of course we want the best for you. And while you're-"

"But that's it. I'm obviously not under your roof. Am I?"

"Where are you?"

"I'm not even in the same city as you." Well, she wouldn't be shortly.

"Where are you? And how did you get there?"

Alyssa laughed bitterly. "You wouldn't believe me if I told you."

"Try me."

"Well, I hooked up with some religious nuts who think they can guard my soul and want me to learn the Lord's Prayer. They think it'll be good for me to know it."

"Don't get smart with me, Alyssa."

Alyssa laughed again. "I said you wouldn't believe me." She saw Riley shake his head out of the corner of her eye. "Here, you can talk to one of them. This is Riley, Mum." She shoved the phone at Riley with a grin.

"Hello, ma'am." There was a pause as Riley listened. "No." Another pause. "We're going on a religious retreat."

Alyssa giggled and ignored the glare Riley sent her. She wished she'd thought to put her phone on speaker mode. Or that she had the guts to press her ear to the phone to hear the other end of the conversation.

"She's eighteen. She doesn't need parental

permission to go on the retreat… you're welcome to do that, but the police will say the same… she chose to join us of her own free will… no, we're not a cult, we're part of a mainstream-" Riley's words were interrupted and he shook his head as he listened. "You can talk to our priest if you want… of course he wouldn't… twenty… no, there'll be separate sleeping accommodation… we don't believe in pre-marital sex."

Alyssa smothered her laughter with her hands.

"My cousin… She's nineteen… Scarlett… It's a family name, ma'am… Grace… no, of course not…yes… I'll encourage her to ring once a day… I don't know what the coverage will be like… I'll look out for her like she's my own sister… it's Allie's choice, but I do understand-" Again his words ended abruptly. "I'm sorry you feel that way… I have to go now… I'm sorry, but-" he sighed as his words were cut off. "I'm sorry… bye." Riley ended the call and handed the phone to Alyssa who continued to grin. "You're lucky I believe in forgiveness."

Alyssa burst out laughing. The first time in what felt like years.

"Alex! Pay attention to the road," Scarlett said sharply.

Alyssa turned her phone off. "I won't be able to ring her every day. My battery's nearly flat."

"Then we'll get a car charger for it," Riley said.

"Great." Alyssa returned the phone to one of the outside pouches of her backpack and pulled her book out. She flicked through until she found the last words she recalled reading before she'd fallen asleep in the church.

Chapter Fifteen

They pulled up in front of a block of flats a couple of streets back from the beach. Alex unplugged the phone from the car charger they'd stopped to buy earlier and handed it to Alyssa. She reluctantly took it.

"So good to get out of the car." Scarlett threw her door open and hopped out, her backpack over one shoulder. Riley and Alex quickly followed her example.

Alyssa continued to sit in the car, even when Alex opened her door. She glanced up as he moved to stand near her. One arm rested across the top of the car door and his shadow fell on her.

"It can't be too comfortable sitting in there."

Alyssa sighed. "You didn't even ring him to say we're coming. What if he's not home?"

"He works nights. He's probably in bed."

"Alex, that's worse. We can't drag him out of bed."

"He's family."

"I thought you said he was out of the family business."

"Yeah, but not being a demon hunter doesn't mean you've left the family. Come on, Alyssa. It's hot out here."

Alyssa pushed him out of the way. They still wore their long sleeved black shirts. She guessed it'd be cruel to make them stand in the heat after all they'd done for her. She followed Scarlett and Riley as they climbed a set of stairs.

Scarlett rapped on the door, waited a few seconds and knocked louder.

"I'm coming. No need to knock the door down," an irate voice called from inside.

Alyssa gasped when the door opened. The arm that held the door caught her gaze. A demon mark travelled all the way to the elbow. The mark had been tattooed to make it look like barbed wire was wrapped around the arm. She finally managed to drag her gaze from the arm to see the owner of it staring at her. Blue eyes, a sharp contrast to the dark hair and tanned skin. It wasn't until then she realised the man was only wearing a pair of shorts sitting low on his hips.

"You look terrible, Blake. The scruffy look doesn't

suit you. Get a haircut and have a shave." Scarlett pushed past her cousin to step inside.

Blake ignored her, his gaze on Alyssa. He grabbed her left arm and turned it so he could look at her wrist. He dropped it instantly. Next he snagged the crimson lock of hair and ran it through his fingers.

Alyssa nearly stopped breathing under the intense scrutiny. She took a deep breath when Blake turned to face Scarlett.

"Get out."

"Aw Blake, don't be like that." Scarlett pulled a chair out from the table and dropped onto it. "We hardly ever get to see you."

"Take your demon touched and get out of here."

Riley stepped inside the apartment and glanced around. "We just need to use your spare room for the day."

"I don't have anything to do with demons," Blake said.

"Really?" Riley moved away from the window ledge he'd run his fingers over. "You salt your ledges for fun do you?"

Scarlett leapt from her chair. "You don't! You have better ways to fight them than that, Blake."

"Don't lecture me, Scarlett." Blake turned back to the doorway and met Alyssa's gaze. "Get inside. And shut the door. I don't what the neighbours knowing my business."

Alyssa stepped inside. Alex followed her. She glanced around the compact apartment. A counter was all that separated the lounge room and kitchen. The kitchen was barely large enough for the square table and four chairs and the lounge room looked crowded with a sofa, television and bookcase.

"So who are you?" Blake demanded.

"Alyssa. Allie."

"Leave her be, Blake." Alex stepped in front of her.

Blake looked between Alyssa and Alex. "I wouldn't have thought her your type."

"That's enough, Blake." Scarlett grabbed Blake by the arm so he'd be forced to look at her. "We need a few hours rest then we'll be out of your way."

"Get a room somewhere then."

"Blake-"

Blake rounded on Riley. "Don't start on me, little brother. I've made my choices. Don't interfere with them. Do you think I want to lose someone else to them?"

"Not hunting them doesn't make them stop existing."

"Yeah, but chasing them isn't going to make your life any longer, Ry."

"Avoiding them won't make your life any safer. Otherwise you wouldn't have salt across the entrances."

"Yeah well, that's my problem. I refuse to watch someone else I love die." He turned towards Alyssa, "And if you were smart, you wouldn't hang around with them either."

"She hasn't got a choice. She's demon bait," Riley said.

"What the-"

"Enough you two. Blake, we just need somewhere to crash for the day. We'll be out of here before dark. We're not asking you to help us hunt demons. We only need somewhere safe to sleep," Scarlett said.

"You're out of here before that demon's on the move again. You get yourself killed, I don't want to see it. I have more than enough nightmares to pick from each night without adding that to the selection."

Riley held up his hands. "That's fine. We'll take off about four. That should give us time to find sanctuary for the night."

"Not one minute later," Blake warned.

"That'll be enough time to rest," Riley said.

Blake waved towards the three closed doors that were on Alyssa's right. "Make yourself at home." He strode towards the kettle sitting on the kitchen bench, checked the water level then turned it on. He grabbed the salt sitting out beside it and threw it towards Riley, who caught it. "Fix my window ledge and the door. I need more sleep."

"It's daylight." Alyssa frowned.

"She doesn't know much, does she?" Blake asked of no one in particular.

"I don't like being talked about like I'm not here." Alyssa's hands went to her hips and she glared at Blake.

Blake shrugged. "I don't like being dragged out of bed when I've only had a few hours sleep. Get over it." He grabbed a cup and spoon from a draining rack filled with clean crockery.

"They don't tell me anything, so how am I meant to know anything?" Alyssa demanded.

"Not my problem." Blake grabbed a jar of coffee and milk from the fridge. "And don't expect me to wait on you. You want a drink, get it yourself." He left everything on the bench and stalked to the sofa as he took a sip of his coffee.

"Bathroom and bed for me." Riley strode towards the middle door.

"Don't know where you all expect to fit," Blake muttered.

"Can she have your room?" Scarlett waved towards Alyssa.

"Don't like her much, do you?" Blake asked Scarlett.

"It'd be unchristian to hate someone," Scarlett said.

"I didn't say you hated her." Blake sipped his coffee. "Who cares. Take over the joint. I'll use the sofa. Just get out of my hair so I can get back to sleep."

Riley came out of the bathroom and went into the door towards the rear of the apartment. Scarlett made her way into the bathroom next. Riley poked his head out of the bedroom door.

"There's only two single beds in here, Blake."

"Swag in the wardrobe."

"Thanks." Riley shut the door again.

Silence descended over the room until Scarlett came out of the bathroom. "Wake me at four, Blake."

"Three-thirty. You're out the door at four."

Scarlett grinned. "To the second, huh?"

"Don't push it, cousin."

Scarlett didn't bother answering. She disappeared inside the room Riley had entered.

"Alyssa?" Alex gestured towards the bathroom.

She nodded and quickly went in and shut the door. She dropped her backpack on the floor and looked around the cramped room. She closed her eyes, refusing to think of the last cramped bathroom she'd been in. She opened her eyes again and focused on the differences. The small chipped mirror above the basin, the skinny linen cupboard that was slightly warped from the moisture, the old fashioned toilet with its single flush and the tiled shower.

She quickly used the bathroom and finished with cleaning off the makeup she'd applied at the service station they'd stopped at for breakfast. She stared at her face where the bruise had once been. The skin was clear. Her gaze dropped to her arms and she ran a finger over a pink line on her left arm. Next her finger gingerly touched her lip. Healed. A shudder went through her as she remembered Retribution's blood spraying her when she'd stabbed him.

Pushing thoughts of demons from her mind, she opened the door. Blake and Alex fell silent. She wondered what they were talking about. She might be getting paranoid, but she had a feeling they'd discussed her.

"Door on your left." Alex moved forward.

"Thanks for letting us stay." Alyssa moved out of the way so Alex could use the bathroom.

"I don't think I had much choice." Blake strode towards the door Alex had indicated. He swung it open and grabbed one of the pillows off the rumpled bed.

"I can use the sofa." Alyssa looked up at Blake as he stood beside her.

Blake shook his head. He reached out and lifted her crimson lock of hair and let it drift from his fingers. "In there's the safest place for demon bait."

"Why?"

Blake tossed his pillow across the room to the couch before he held up his left arm. "This is like a neon sign letting all the demons wandering around know I'm here. I've made protecting my bedroom a priority."

Alyssa reached out to touch the demon mark. Her fingers never made contact. Blake grabbed her by the wrist with his right hand as he dropped his left. His gaze met hers. "Have you heard about the downside of curiosity, Allie Cat?"

Alyssa's mouth went dry as she continued to stare up at him.

Blake let go of her suddenly and stepped away. "Get some sleep."

Alyssa licked her lips, and swallowed shakily. "Scarlett's wrong. The scruffy look does suit you." Before her lips had finished curving into a smile, she'd closed the door. She grinned at the second of surprise she'd seen on Blake's face. A pity we aren't staying longer than the day, she thought as she moved towards the rumpled bed. It'd been ages since she'd met someone who made her blood warm just by looking at them.

She dropped the backpack on the floor and removed her boots. She lay across the queen-sized bed, pulled the remaining pillow to her and snuggled into it. The dark curtains kept most of the light out. She rolled onto her stomach. The bed was comfortable and smelled faintly of Blake. Alyssa tried to close her eyes. She rolled onto her back and watched the ceiling fan spin lazily. The room was small. A built-in wardrobe at the foot of the bed, a small bookcase crammed with books on one wall and two bedside cabinets. She rolled onto her side. Then the other.

She turned on the lamp as she rose from the bed and paced in the narrow space. She continued her pacing even when she heard a door open, the sound of low voices and then the door shut again.

A sharp rap on her door and it swung open. Blake stood in the doorway. "Lie down and go to sleep. You're keeping everyone awake."

"I can't."

"You can and will. Alex won't sleep while he thinks you need someone to watch over you."

"Do I need someone to watch over me while I sleep?"

"No. It's safe here. No minor demon can enter."

"But that's the problem. It isn't a minor demon." Alyssa walked towards Blake, stopping just in front of him. "Can you keep the powerful ones out?"

"I don't have to. It's daytime. Go to sleep and stop playing games."

"Games! You think this is a game? I could die tonight!"

Blake stepped into the room and shut the door so Alyssa was forced to take a step back. "Keep your voice down. People are trying to sleep."

"Yeah, well aren't they lucky."

"They're doing their best to keep you alive. Show some consideration."

"Excuse me if I don't fall to my knees in gratitude. I've been preoccupied lately. I have this little problem of seeing blood and demons every time I close my eyes. Hell! I don't even need to close them."

When Alyssa would have turned away from Blake, he grabbed her shoulder and stepped in close. "You don't know what nightmares are yet, Allie Cat."

"And you do?"

"Do you know how old someone in my family usually is when they get marks as long as mine? Forty to fifty years old. And I have them at twenty-two. Twenty-two! I had them before I'd turned twenty-one. Do you want me to tell you what it takes to get them that fast? You want me to tell you every little gory detail? I can tell you all about blood."

Alyssa placed a hand against Blake's bare chest. "Blake, I-"

"Spare me." It was his turn to move away.

Alyssa took a couple of steps and placed her hand on his back. "I-" she stepped back hurriedly as Blake spun to face her, his eyes blazing.

"Back off, Allie."

"It wasn't my choice to come here. I don't know how you got those marks. No one tells me anything."

"Let's just say the one I was supposed to protect didn't make it."

Alyssa's eyes widened and she started to tremble.

"Aw hell. I'm sorry, Allie Cat." Blake wrapped his arms around her. He pressed her head to his chest.

Alyssa closed her eyes, the beat of his heart in her ears. Another shudder went through her and his hand started to make lazy movements across her back. She didn't find them comforting, but they did make her feel alive. She lifted her head and rose on tiptoes. Her lips met his. For a few seconds Blake returned her kiss before he pushed her from him.

"You're more dangerous than demons, Allie."

Alyssa shook her head and took a step forward.

"No. I live by my family's beliefs." Blake held up his left arm and laughed harshly. "How can I do otherwise?"

"What's that supposed to mean? I don't know your family's beliefs." Alyssa ran her hand along the mark. "Why barbed wire?"

"Call it my rebellion against the family business. I can't go back to fighting demons unless I want these tattoos to be as crimson as your hair." He dropped his arm, his right hand capturing hers. "What are you trying to do?"

"I thought that'd be obvious. I could be dead before morning."

"Then I'd think you'd be taking a little better care of your soul."

"I don't believe in your religious crap."

"I do. It's not going to happen, Allie."

"Why?"

"Because we don't believe in sex outside the bonds of marriage."

"You're a virgin?" Alyssa stared at him in disbelief.

"I'm human Allie, not a saint."

"What's that supposed to mean?"

"Mind your own damned business. How about I ask the same of you? You a virgin, Allie Cat? Or did curiosity get the better of you?"

Alyssa shook her head, unable to meet his gaze.

"What's that supposed to mean? Yes you are, or no you aren't?"

"Yes," she whispered.

"Thank God for small mercies."

Startled, Alyssa met his gaze again. "What?"

"A few less sins'll make it easier for them to protect you."

"Sin! Sex is not a sin. You're so old fashioned."

Blake shrugged. "I don't attack your beliefs."

"I don't have any."

"That's a belief in itself."

Alyssa frowned. "That doesn't make sense."

"It doesn't have to. It just is." Blake turned away from her.

"Where are you going?"

"To sleep."

"You might as well have your bed back. I can't sleep."

"Get in the bed, Allie."

"No."

"Allie."

"You can't make me go to sleep." Her chin rose and she glared at him. She was sick of being ordered around.

"You're not going out there to wander around, make noise and keep everyone awake. Alex'll feel obligated to sit with you and keep you company."

"I don't need company."

"Too bad." Blake advanced on her and Alyssa retreated.

"Fine. But you can't keep me in it." Alyssa dropped onto the bed.

"Move over."

"Why?"

"Can't you do anything without questioning it?"

"Probably not."

"Too bad. Now shove over." Blake lifted her feet off the floor and dropped them on the bed. Alyssa moved out of the way when she saw Blake was serious.

"I'm not sleeping next to you."

"You were willing to do more than that a minute ago."

"I changed my mind."

"Good." Blake grabbed the pillow and rolled onto his side, his back to her. He reached out and turned off the lamp.

"I don't have a pillow."

"Shut up, Allie Cat. I'm tired."

Alyssa muttered under her breath. She lay on her back and stared at the ceiling fan. She yawned. She listened to the soft sounds of Blake breathing beside her and her eyes started to close.

Chapter Sixteen

A soft noise woke Alyssa and her eyes opened. She turned her head, which now rested on Blake's chest. Her gaze fell on Alex who stood frozen in the doorway. Before she could say anything, he turned away.

The closing door woke Blake. He pushed Alyssa from him and sat up. "Tell me that wasn't Alex." When Alyssa didn't answer, he swore.

"I-"

"You're a menace. You should come with a health warning."

"I didn't invite you into the bed," Alyssa hissed.

Blake smiled, but his eyes remained serious. "Really? I seem to clearly recall-"

"I took that offer back."

"Yeah well, that doesn't help. Now listen for a

change. Stay in here. Give me some time to talk to him. Think you can manage that?"

"Yes." She spoke through clenched teeth.

Blake strode towards his wardrobe and slid the door open. He grabbed a shirt off a coat hanger and pulled it on. He didn't bother with the buttons. Next he grabbed a pair of black jeans and pulled them on over his shorts. "Stay." He strode from the room and let the door shut softly.

"Stay! I'm not a bloody dog," Alyssa muttered.

She rose from the bed and walked over to the bookcase. The room was too dim for reading titles so she strode to the lamp. At the last second she changed her mind and pulled the curtain to the side. She dropped it into place, her hand going to her heart that raced rapidly in her chest.

"No," she moaned. "Impossible."

She hesitantly reached out to the curtain again. This time she only drew it enough apart to peek outside. Parked beside their car was Nathan's. He sat in the passenger seat, Eric beside him in the driver's seat. He flipped shut the laptop he held and pointed towards Blake's apartment. Alyssa backed away from the window and stumbled over her boots. She quickly pulled them on and grabbed the gun from her backpack. If it was only Nathan, they might've been able to take him. But two of them with guns made it too risky. And Nathan was sure to have more guns. She threw the bedroom door open.

"I thought I told you-" Blake broke off, his gaze drawn to the gun in her hand. "What the hell are you doing running around with that?"

"Nathan."

"Impossible." Alex strode to the kitchen window. He swore.

"Alex!" Scarlett came out of the bathroom in time to hear him, stopping beside Alyssa.

"Nathan," Alex muttered.

Scarlett turned to Blake. "I don't suppose there's a back way out of here."

Blake shook his head. "Who's Nathan?"

"He's the one who wants to give me to a demon. And he has Eric with him this time. He was driving the car for Nathan the first night," Alyssa said.

"He's got to get through us first," Alex said. "Go back to the bedroom, Allie."

"No."

"Don't be so stubborn." Alex glared at her.

"Forget it. Her head. If she doesn't want your help, you can't force it on her," Blake said.

Riley came out of the bedroom, pulling a t-shirt

on. He stopped and glanced around at them. His gaze zeroed in on the gun. "What's happening?"

"Nathan," Scarlett said. Her words were followed by footsteps coming up the stairs and a knock on the door.

Blake moved quietly towards Scarlett and whispered, "How did he find you? This place isn't even listed in my name. I took it over from a friend."

Scarlet shrugged.

Riley moved close to them so they could hear his whisper. "It must be the guns."

"Guns? There's more than one?" Blake asked.

Riley nodded. There was a harder knock on the door as Alex moved close.

Blake rubbed his forehead. "Okay. Get the other gun." He spoke softly enough Nathan wouldn't hear.

Riley nodded and retreated to the spare room.

Blake turned to Scarlett. "My bedroom. Backpack in the bottom of the wardrobe. Get it."

Scarlett saluted with a partially suppressed grin before she disappeared into the bedroom. The next knock sounded louder.

"Give me the gun." Blake held out his hand. Alyssa shook her head. "Don't be so dammed stupid. Give me the gun and get in the spare room. Let's get out of here in one piece."

Alyssa reluctantly handed over the gun. Riley came out of the bedroom and gave Blake the other gun.

"Riley, roll up my swag. Alex, abseiling rope in the bottom of the wardrobe in the spare room. And all of you stay in there." Blake moved to the kitchen table and placed the two guns gently on it.

Alyssa hovered in the doorway of the spare bedroom and watched as he grabbed a set of keys hung by the front door and held them tightly so they didn't rattle. He glanced towards the door that shook with the impatient knock. Scarlett came out of the bedroom with Blake and Alyssa's backpacks. Blake pointed to the spare bedroom and she nodded before she headed there. Alyssa stepped back so Blake could close and lock the door of the spare bedroom.

Blake beckoned Riley to him and pointed to the floor. "Let me know the minute they're in."

Riley nodded and lay at the door so he could watch under it.

Alex was at the window removing the insect screen. He handed it to Scarlett who put it in the built-in wardrobe. She took the car keys Blake handed her and tucked them in her pocket.

"You first." Blake squeezed Scarlett's shoulder.

Scarlett nodded and moved to the window. She stepped into the harness and climbed onto the window ledge. Alex lowered her down until her feet touched on the industrial bin below the window. She quickly undid the harness and Alex hauled it up. Alex helped Alyssa into the harness next while Blake dropped the backpacks down to Scarlett. Riley joined them at the window as Alyssa reached the bin.

"What's happening up there?" Alyssa demanded of Scarlett.

"I know as much as you do." Scarlett watched as Riley was lowered.

"What's happening?" Alyssa asked the moment Riley was close enough.

"They're in. Headed straight for the table where we put the guns." Riley undid the harness so it could be drawn up.

Alyssa looked up at the window where Blake and Alex spoke quietly. They clasped, left hands against forearms so their wrists touched. Then Blake lowered Alex to the bin. He let the rope fall after him.

"Alex! No! We can't leave him up there." Alyssa grabbed his arm. She looked up at the window and Blake smiled at her. She glared up at him.

"Move off the bin. Scarlett, spread the swag out on it." Alex jumped off the bin. "Quickly."

"It's too far," Alyssa protested.

"Stop arguing, Allie." Riley handed her backpack to her. He pulled his own on.

Alex grabbed Alyssa's hand and tugged her towards the side of the building. "Hurry up. We need to get Blake's vehicle." He held out his hand to Scarlett who dropped the keys into his open hand.

"But what about Blake?" Alyssa asked.

"He can't jump until we're safe. Too much noise. Come on, Alyssa." Alex tugged on her hand to hurry her up.

"You should've said." She broke into a run.

They stopped at a four-wheel-drive similar to the one Alyssa had first seen them driving. Alex pressed the central locking button and they piled in. He started the vehicle and drove to the back of the building where he reversed up to the industrial bin.

"Open the door and move over here, Allie," Riley said.

Alyssa swung the door open as she watched Blake land on the bin. He moved to the side, rolled the swag in one fluid movement, hefted it and leapt to the ground. He shoved it into the back of the vehicle and climbed in. He'd barely shut the door when Alex drove forward. Alyssa looked out the rear window and saw first Nathan and then Eric framed in the window.

"They're going to catch us." Alyssa couldn't take her gaze from the rear window.

Chapter Seventeen

Blake pulled his phone from a pocket in his jeans. "Alex, take the second street on the left. Then the first on the right." He pressed the button for his address book as he spoke. He hit dial when he found the correct entry. "Dale… Open the garage door… Thanks mate." He ended the call and put the phone back in his pocket. "Okay, slow down. It's the house up here with the rusted car out the front. Go down beside it. There's a garage out the back. Should be open."

It was being opened as they drove around behind the house. A skinny man with long hair, torn jeans and a cigarette hanging out his mouth pulled the roller door shut behind them.

Alex turned off the engine. "Interesting company you keep."

Blake grinned. "I work with him."

"No one's mentioned where you work," Alyssa said.

"Night club." Blake opened the door and hopped out of the vehicle.

The side door of the garage opened and Dale stepped inside. "So what are you hiding from?" His gaze landed on Alyssa as she joined Blake. "Ahh, nice." He grinned at her and stepped forward, offering his hand. "Dale. And who are you, gorgeous?"

Blake dropped an arm around Alyssa's shoulders. "This is Allie. My cousins, Scarlett and Alex. And my brother, Riley." Blake glanced at each of them as they joined him.

"No problem," Dale grinned as he took a step back. "So, why you hiding out?"

"Allie's ex has a problem with letting go. And he likes to settle things with guns," Blake said.

"Nasty. You want to come up to the house? Beat sitting around in here waiting for him to disappear." Dale gestured towards the open door.

Blake shook his head. "Better not risk it. We'll be out of here around dark." He squeezed Alyssa's shoulder when she was about to protest. "Thanks for this, mate."

"No problem." Dale shrugged. "Hey, I owe you one. This might go a little way to evening things."

"A long way," Blake said.

"All right then. Well, I'm up at the house if you need me. Nice meeting you all." Dale flicked on the light switch before he pulled the door closed behind him.

As soon as Dale had left, Alyssa turned on Blake. "I thought you lot didn't believe in lying."

Blake shrugged. "I kept fairly close to the truth. Sometimes a lie can save a life."

"And what do you mean by waiting till dark to leave? We've got to be out of here before dark. What about the demon?" Alyssa demanded.

"It'll take him a bit to hunt you down. I can have you at a sanctuary within twenty minutes," Blake said.

"There's no church that close," Scarlett said.

"Graveyard."

"It's hallowed?" Alex asked.

Blake nodded. "Yeah." He rubbed his left arm. "So what do you want to do while we wait? I've got a deck of cards." He turned to Alyssa. "You up for a game of strip poker?"

"Blake!"

Blake laughed at Scarlett's warning tone. "She won't say yes. No one has goaded her into it yet."

Alyssa turned away from Blake. She grabbed her backpack out of the vehicle and strode to the other side. Alex fell in beside her.

"He doesn't mean anything by it, Allie. He jokes around to cope, like Riley does. I guess in the eighteen months he's been away from the family his jokes have become a little off colour."

"Forget it, Alex. I'm not letting it bother me."

"I'm sorry about before."

"When?" Alyssa spied a dusty bench seat and after a half-hearted swipe at it with her hand, sat down.

Alex sat beside her. "When I came into the bedroom this morning. Blake explained you were having trouble sleeping. You were thinking of the demon. He said he fell asleep waiting for you to go to sleep."

Alyssa glanced at Alex, then towards Blake. She couldn't see him. The vehicle was in the way. "Yeah."

"You could've come and got me. I would've sat up with you."

"You needed sleep. Did you sleep at the church?"

"Yeah. Riley and Scarlett took turns watching Nathan with me."

"I should have too."

"What?"

"You should have woken me so I could've taken a turn watching Nathan. I'm not useless, Alex."

"I never-"

"No. But you act like I am."

"Sorry."

"Will a graveyard work?"

"Yeah."

"I thought demons hung out in them."

Alex smiled fleetingly. "That'd be spirits. Demons can't step onto holy ground."

Alyssa tried to return his smile.

Alex linked his fingers through hers. "It'll all turn out well. I'll see to it."

Alyssa looked at their hands, his larger than hers. "Can you promise me that?" When Alex remained silent, she looked up. Her gaze collided with his. He looked away. "I didn't think so." She tugged her hand free and stood up. She dusted off the back of her jeans and looked around. She had nowhere to go. Not until night fell.

Alex stood up. "Alyssa-"

She turned to face him. "No. I just can't talk any more. What I really want is to be looking forward to the weekend. To be thinking about going out Friday night to a nightclub with friends. And when I'm there I want to have a few drinks, dance until my feet feel like they might explode and then go home and crawl into bed and wake up when the day's half done. I'm meant to be starting uni next year. I'm young. I should be out having fun, not wondering when I'll die. I want to be able to wake in the morning and think the world's a good place. Not know it's filled with all kinds of horror."

"The world is a good place."

"How can you say that? It's complete and utter crap."

"Alyssa–"

"Demons, for god's sake! How much worse can it get?"

"A lot worse," Blake said quietly.

Alyssa spun to face him. She hadn't heard him join them.

"Blake–"

Blake cut Alex's words off. "Join Riley and Scarlett." When Alex was about to argue, Blake snapped, "Now, Alex. You're making the situation worse."

Alex shot one last anguished look at Alyssa before he turned away. Feeling guilty for what she'd heaped on him, Alyssa reached out to Alex and opened her mouth to call him back. Blake grabbed her forearm before she made contact and spun her to face him.

Blake moved close so his mouth was near her ear. "Do you enjoy chewing him up and spitting him out?"

"I–"

"He's tearing himself up trying to make this easier on you. Don't you care?"

"Of course I do." Alyssa kept her voice equally quiet. She turned her head slightly so she could look him in the eye. Their lips were a breath apart. "But he isn't the one the demon's after."

"He's the one the demon'll have to get through before it can get to you."

"I told them not–"

"Are you always this dense? What do you think the chances are any one of them'll stand aside and let the demon get you?"

Alyssa gasped, her eyes widening. "They won't." She tried to pull away, but Blake's grip tightened on her forearm. "Let me go. I've got to get out of here."

"What are you going to do? Sacrifice yourself?"

"Yes. No. I don't know. I can't let them kill themselves because of me."

"Then let them do their job. They know what

they're doing. All you have to do is shut up, listen and follow orders. How hard can that be?"

Alyssa laughed abruptly. "How hard? How about so difficult it's the reason I ended up in this situation in the first place. Don't you laugh at me."

Blake continued to grin at her. "Figures."

Alyssa reached up and ran her fingers across his cheek, the stubble rough against her fingers. "You should smile more often."

Blake's smile vanished. He pulled her hand from his face. "You can't help it, can you? Keep your hands to yourself."

Alyssa glanced down to where his hand held her. "Like you do?" She met his gaze again and refused to look away even with how uncomfortable his intense stare made her feel.

Blake released her and stepped back a fraction. "Think you can manage for one night to do exactly as you're told without question?"

"I'll try."

Blake shook his head. "Not the answer I was looking for."

"I can only try. Don't they say a leopard can't change his spots?"

"Sometimes, Allie Cat, a leopard needs to change

her spots before she becomes a rug on someone's floor." Blake turned his head.

Alyssa turned to see what had caught his attention. Scarlett walked towards them. Alyssa was surprised by the look Scarlett sent her. It didn't go hand in hand with her belief in forgiving others.

"What're we going to do about dinner?" Scarlett faced Blake and ignored Alyssa after that single look.

Blake rubbed his forehead. He sighed heavily. "I've got it under control. There's a camp table and four camp chairs in the back of the four-wheel-drive. Picnic set too. Have Alex set it up. I'm sure he could do with the distraction."

"That's a lot of gear to be carting around. Some habits are hard to break, huh?" Scarlett grinned at him.

"Apparently."

"What can I do?" Alyssa asked.

"I think you've done enough for today." Scarlett didn't even look at her.

"Scarlett." There was a warning in Blake's tone.

"Sorry, Blake. You're right. I guess we're all on edge." Scarlett ran her fingers through her short hair.

"That's understandable." Blake reached out to rest his hand on Scarlett's shoulder for a moment.

"It's not just that. I don't think we're the right ones for this job."

"Who said you were?"

"Gran. But then a lot of the family aren't at home. More than half of them are out of the country. It's not like she had a lot of candidates to choose from."

"Gran would've left her be if she didn't think you could cope. Family's always come first for Gran," Blake said.

Alyssa stood quietly and soaked up every piece of information. Even her initial rush of anger at Scarlett's words had evaporated at the thought of learning more of what was going on.

"I guess." Scarlett glanced towards Alyssa. "But all Gran would've focused on was the demon and if we could handle it."

"Yeah well, I'm here now. That'll completely change the equation," Blake said.

"Blake," Scarlett hesitated. "We don't expect you to stay with us. We know you don't want to be part of this. I'm sorry we came to you this morning. It wasn't meant to go like this."

Blake momentarily pressed a finger to Scarlett's lips. "Shh. I'm glad you came. Maybe it's time I laid old ghosts to rest."

"Really?" Scarlett appeared to be on the edge of smiling.

Blake smiled. "Really. Now go and get Alex to set the table."

Scarlett started to move away, then turned back. "What else have you got in there?"

"Tent, camp stove, cookware, some tinned and dried goods." Blake shrugged. "The usual stuff."

"Good. But we'll have to go back to the car at some stage to get our swords for tonight. Just in case."

Blake frowned, then grinned. "How fond are you of your stereo?"

Scarlett frowned. "Is that a trick question?"

Blake laughed. "Don't worry about it. Dinner and swords. They'll be here within the hour."

Scarlett stared at him for a moment. "Why is it I feel concern at that comment?"

"Because you like to worry. Go on. I have some calls to make." Blake pulled out his phone.

Scarlett nodded and strode away.

Blake turned to Alyssa. "Anything you don't like on pizza?"

"Most things."

"Seriously?"

"I like meat lovers."

Blake hit the send button and started to move away

from Alyssa. All she heard was his greeting to Dale. She glared at his back and wished she could follow and find out what was going on. A few minutes later, he walked past her to the personal access door. Dale met him there. Alyssa wandered closer even though she knew she wouldn't be in time to hear the conversation. But she did see Blake give Dale fifty dollars.

Chapter Eighteen

Dale returned within an hour with pizza and the swords in their case. Their meal was a quiet affair. None of them seemed to feel like talking. Especially once it began to grow dark outside. By the time it was completely dark, everything was back in the vehicle and Dale pushed up the roller door. They stood back as Blake talked with Dale.

"I'm not sure when I'll be back. I rang work, so there might even be some extra shifts," Blake said.

"Thanks. I'll ask the boss. I forgot to tell you earlier. Your door was shut at your apartment. Doesn't mean it was locked. I'll send one of the guys over later to check on that." Dale grinned. "One of the ones whose fingers aren't so light."

"I appreciate that." Blake held out his right hand. "I'll let you know when I'm back. But if you can keep an eye on the place until then?"

"Sure thing."

Blake turned away and went first to Alex for the car keys and then hopped in the driver's seat.

"I'm in the front," Scarlett told Alex as she walked past him.

Riley threw an arm around Alex's shoulder. "That's okay, cuz. I don't mind you sitting in the back with me."

"I'm sure I should feel honoured," Alex said dryly.

Alyssa trailed behind them. She felt like an outsider. She felt a little better when Alex held the door open and waited for her to hop in. Once she was buckled, she noticed a phone car charger that looked very familiar. "That's-" she shook her head.

Blake glanced at her using the rear view mirror and then looked down. He chuckled and turned to face her. "Riley mentioned you needed it so you could reluctantly keep in touch with your parents. Dale brought it over when he brought the swords."

"Gee, thanks, Riley," Alyssa said.

Riley grinned at her. "Any time, Allie."

They fell silent again as Blake reversed the vehicle and waved to Dale who pulled the roller door down once they were out. With her mind already on her phone, Alyssa pulled it out and turned it on.

Erin answered on the first ring. "You owe me big time, girl."

"I know."

"Good. By the time you get home I should've figured out the price."

Alyssa laughed. She could count the days she and Erin hadn't spoken to each other. "Miss you, Erin."

"Yeah well, you were the one who decided to take off, not me."

"Yeah." She hesitated. "Have you seen Nathan again?"

"No. Well, I don't think so. But that dude that was driving, I thought I saw him. It's all your fault. I had nightmares about you getting into that car. Now I'm seeing Nathan and that other one."

"Eric."

"Whatever. Just don't do anything as stupid as that again. Okay?"

"Okay." Alyssa hoped that was all it was. Erin seeing things she was worried about. But she didn't really believe that. Scarlett better have a tonne of people watching Erin and her parents.

"And what's this your mum told mine about you being on a religious retreat? Surely they didn't get that right."

Alyssa couldn't help laughing at her friend's tone. "It seemed the easiest way to explain things."

"So you aren't really then? I knew it couldn't be right. I mean, you're an atheist, right?"

"Your guess is as good as mine." Suddenly even a smile seemed too much of an effort.

"You know you can tell me anything, don't you? Even if it's completely off the wall, I'll believe you."

"How completely off the wall?"

"Anything. Even alien abduction," Erin assured her.

"Thanks, Erin."

"So… you're not on an alien spaceship are you?"

"No. But what do you know about demons?"

"Horns, forked tail, cloven hooves and fire engine red?"

"Something like that."

"Ah… Allie, you're scaring me again."

"Yeah, me too." There was silence between them before Alyssa spoke again. "Erin, I've got to go."

"Where are you?"

"You'd never believe me."

"Try me."

Alyssa took a deep breath. "We've just arrived at a graveyard."

"What the hell are you getting yourself into, Allie?"

"Aiming for the opposite of that."

"Well aim a little harder. Don't you dare let anything happen to yourself. You're the sister Mum and Dad were meant to give me."

"I know, Erin. I feel the same way. I'll call you tomorrow."

"Are you in danger?"

"Erin, I have to go."

"Call me every hour."

"Erin!"

"Fine. I won't be able to sleep at all until I hear from you."

"I shouldn't have said anything to you."

"Yes you should. Allie, come home."

Alyssa looked over at Riley who held out his hand. "Ah, Erin. Someone wants to talk to you. Riley."

"What for?"

"How would I know?"

"Okay." Erin sighed heavily.

Alyssa handed the phone to Riley who promptly hopped out of the vehicle. He moved away from her and Alyssa would have followed if Blake hadn't grabbed her by the arm.

"Let me go."

"Don't be dense, Allie Cat. He walked off for a reason."

Alyssa glared at Blake. "Yeah, but he's talking to my friend."

"Who you were trying to scare witless by the sounds of it."

"I wasn't. We tell each other everything. She's the sister of my heart."

"Then let my brother reassure her that we'll take care of you."

Alyssa glanced over to Riley, outlined by moonlight, as he sat on the fence that edged the graveyard. "Okay," she whispered. "But I do need to ask him if they've still got people watching Erin and my parents."

"No you don't." Blake smiled momentarily. "Nice excuse though. And yes, there's still people watching them. Scarlett told me." He paused. "Come on. Help me find a comfortable place to wait for Nathan. There are torches in the back."

Alex was at the back of the vehicle, the swag on his shoulder, a torch in his hand and his backpack on. Scarlett stood a few paces away with a picnic blanket and another torch. Blake handed Alyssa a torch and then shifted some of the gear in the back of his vehicle forward so he could lift the floor panel. On top of the spare wheel was a sword in a scabbard.

Scarlett laughed when she saw him pull it out. "Give up, huh?"

Blake ran his hand over the hilt. "It's been in there since I left."

"Blake-" Scarlett's laughter evaporated immediately.

"Shh. As Gran says, I choose which path my feet tread." Blake closed the back door and then turned to Alyssa. "Grab your backpack and let's go."

They set up under an old tree. Scarlett was given the swag and told to take a rest while Alex, Alyssa and Blake sat on the picnic blanket.

"Please tell me there's something we can do other than watch stars," Alyssa said.

"I've got that deck of cards no one wanted to use earlier," Blake said.

"Hardly seems a fair game when I'm hopeless at poker." Alyssa stared at Blake, but his face was little more than shadows.

There was amusement in Blake's voice when he replied. "I guess we could always play Strip Jack."

"Does that involve the removal of any clothes?"

Riley joined them in time to hear Alyssa's last comment, a lantern in his hand. He handed her phone to her before he turned to his brother with a grin. "What's it with you and the removal of women's clothes these days? Sounds like you've been working in nightclubs too long."

"Probably." Blake pulled the cards from his backpack. "All in?" He glanced around the circle.

"I'm not agreeing to anything until I know the details," Alyssa said.

Blake continued to shuffle the cards as he stared at her. "Remember that, Allie Cat. That's good advice to live by." Alyssa started to get to her feet. "Sit down, Allie."

"I'm not-"

"Leopard rug?" Blake mocked.

Alyssa's lips thinned. "Fine. Explain your bloody game." When Blake continued to watch her, she demanded, "Well?"

Blake's lips slowly formed a smile. "We might survive this after all, Allie Cat."

Alyssa tried to ignore the good feeling his words and smile gave her. She tried to hang onto her earlier annoyance. By the time they were about ten minutes into their game, it was forgotten.

Alyssa placed a Jack on the pile. She glanced towards Blake who held four cards in his hand. "Your turn." She couldn't resist a grin as he turned over a four of clubs and had to pick up the pile of cards. Her smile vanished and she clutched her stomach.

"Allie Cat?" Blake dropped his cards to reach for her, one hand going to her forehead.

She shook her head, her cards scattered in her lap. Then she bent in two and screamed at the pain that shot through her.

Blake drew her onto his lap. "Riley?"

"He's found her blood."

Blake swore. "Why didn't you warn me, Ry?" He tightened his arms around Alyssa and rocked her as she screamed again. "Alex, there's a bucket in the back of my vehicle." He pulled the keys from his pocket as he tried to hold Alyssa while she groaned and writhed.

Alex grabbed the keys and sprinted for the vehicle.

"How much blood?" Blake demanded.

"I didn't think it was much, but I'm not sure," Riley said.

"We'll find out soon enough," Scarlett said as Alex ran back towards them. She'd joined them at the first scream.

"Blake," Alyssa gasped.

"Shh, I know."

"You don't know." Alyssa screamed again. She tried to push away from Blake. She wanted to curl up and die.

Alex squatted beside them, the bucket held in front

of him. Riley finished rummaging through his backpack and pulled out a vial, a bottle of water and a cup. He added a splash of water to the cup, a few drops from the vial and then held the cup out to Blake.

"You've got to listen to me, Allie Cat."

"Go away," Alyssa moaned. The burning fire stabbed at her again.

"I have a cure for this," Blake whispered against her forehead. "You have to drink this cup."

"I can't." Alyssa clutched at her stomach.

"Come on, Allie. That's an order." He pushed her hair away from her face and looked up at Riley.

Riley held the cup to her lips and tilted it so she could drink. Once she'd drunk the couple of mouthfuls, she pushed the cup away and screamed. She turned tear filled eyes to Blake.

"Sorry," Blake murmured. He helped her sit forward as another intense pain shot through her. This time she gagged and Alex held the bucket in front of her. Blake held her hair out of the way as she threw up the water she'd drunk.

Scarlett leaned forward with a damp cloth as soon as Alex pulled the bucket away. Alyssa moaned and collapsed in Blake's arms. She felt the cool cloth on her face again and she took hold of it to wipe her mouth. She tried to pull away when she saw the dark stain on the cloth.

"Everything's fine, Allie Cat."

"Blood." Alyssa continued to stare at the cloth. "Blake?" Her voice rose.

His arms tightened around her. "You have a blood tie with the demon. He found some more of your blood. We gave you holy water to mute the link. While he felt a rush of pleasure when he consumed your blood, you felt pain." Blake glanced into the bucket. "Maybe an eighth of a cup. Not as bad as I feared."

"Why fear?" Alyssa felt drained.

"Because the more of your blood he consumes the more of his power he can bring through into this world."

"This blood?"

"Alex will dispose of it properly. You trust him to do that?"

"Yes." Alyssa's eyes closed. "Thank you." She fell silent for a moment. "How?" She heard the sound of Blake's laughter rumble in his chest where her ear was pressed.

"You must be doing okay if you're curious, Allie Cat."

"How?" Alyssa opened her eyes to stare up at his shadowy face.

"Fire. It cleanses. Let me put you on the swag so you can have a rest."

Alyssa clutched at Blake's shirt. "Don't leave me."

"Shh. I'll stay with you." Blake lifted her and several cards fell to the ground. He carried her the few steps to the swag. He sat beside her and Alyssa grabbed his right hand and linked her fingers through it. She held it against her chest. His left hand gently stroked her hair back from her forehead.

"I hope you know what you're doing, Blake," Riley said.

"I do too, Ry." Blake sighed. "Where was her blood? How long are we likely to have?"

"About half an hour," Riley said.

"Longer." When the two of them looked towards her, Scarlett said, "Nathan's sure to call the demon to tell him where she is. He'll misjudge how long the demon'll need because he won't know about the blood. I'd say we have at least an hour. Possibly longer."

"Good," Alyssa whispered before she drifted off to sleep.

Chapter Nineteen

"Wake up, Allie Cat."

Alyssa blinked up at the shadow over her. She reached up and ran her fingers along the stubbled cheek, ending her exploration at his lips. She smiled when he lightly nipped them.

"No time for playing, Allie Cat," Blake said softly.

"Then what is it time for?"

"Hide and seek."

"What?" Alyssa sat up and Blake moved back so she could.

Blake held out his hand. "Trust me?"

Alyssa glanced around. Alex, Riley and Scarlett stood a few metres away. They had their backpacks on, a torch in their hands and the lantern was on the ground between her and them. She looked back to Blake, decision made. She placed her hand in his and let him pull her to her feet.

The moment she moved off the swag, Riley rolled it up and hoisted it onto his shoulder. The three of them walked towards the vehicle with all the gear except a single torch Blake held. They even took Blake and Alyssa's backpacks with them.

"What's going on?" Alyssa demanded. "Where are they going?"

"The demon can only track you. He can't come into the graveyard, but Nathan can. So we're going to play hide and seek. We'll stay in the middle of the graveyard and when dawn's getting closer we'll aim for the place I've organised to meet the others at and hopefully Nathan'll be at the opposite end of the graveyard then. And if we're lucky the weather will continue to cooperate with plenty of cloud cover."

"He has guns."

"I know. But we have the advantage."

"And what's that?"

"I know this place. I've wandered it in both daylight and dark. Even in the rain. I moved into that apartment because sanctuary was so close. I won't let him get you, Allie Cat."

"This morning I could've sworn you'd have tossed me to the first demon that came along."

Blake laughed. "I was tired. Lack of sleep makes me

cranky. Come on. Didn't you ever play hide and seek as a kid?"

"I was never very good at it."

"Let me guess, you'd get impatient and check to see where everyone was."

Alyssa laughed. "How'd you know?"

"Don't worry, I'll teach you patience."

"There are other things I'd rather you taught me."

"I know, Allie Cat. Make do with what I'm willing to teach you."

"For now."

"That'll do. Come on then." He tugged on her hand and she followed.

* * *

"This is not my idea of a good hiding place," Alyssa whispered her face nearly against Blake's. They lay facing each other beside an unkempt grave that had a short metal fence around it. The ground was sunken and Alyssa tried not to think about the reason why. "I'm visualising bony hands reaching out and dragging me into that grave."

"I think you've been watching too many horror movies."

Alyssa shuddered. "I don't care what it's from, just take my mind off my thoughts."

"Nice try, Allie Cat."

"Blake, I'm serious. You might not be worried about evil in this graveyard, but I've reached my limit. If I have to lie beside one more broken grave, I swear I'm going to beg Nathan to take me out of here. Every little sound makes me want to scream. I've never liked graveyards." Not to mention the regular threats Nathan had called out were getting to her. They had better have someone really good watching over Erin.

"I'm sorry. I'd swap sides with you, but they're too close."

"Blake, please."

"You're asking more than I'm capable of giving."

"So are you." Alyssa wished she could see his expression, and then she was immediately grateful she couldn't since it meant they were hidden in the shadows.

"Allie Cat." Blake moved forward, his lips brushing hers.

Alyssa closed her eyes, her hand drawn to his chest as she savoured the warmth that filled her. When he pulled away, Alyssa followed and made a noise of protest.

"Allie. Have pity on me." Blake pressed a kiss against her forehead.

Alyssa wriggled closer, her lips curving into a smile

as his arms tightened around her. She'd give him his pity, for now. With her eyes closed and surrounded by Blake's warmth, she started to drift off to sleep. She almost jerked upright when Blake whispered near her ear.

"Time to move again."

Alyssa groaned.

"Final move. Getting close to daylight."

"How do you know?"

"My arm." Blake pressed his fingers against her lips. "No time for questions."

Alyssa kissed the fingers he held there and smiled as he quickly pulled them away.

They crouched low and slowly made their way across the graveyard with trees, headstones and monuments to hide their progress. They sat with their backs pressed against a large tree when they reached the other end.

Alyssa held onto Blake's hand. "I hope you're praying he stays at the other end of the graveyard."

"Like you wouldn't believe."

"Oh, I'd believe. Right now I'm wondering why I never learned any prayers for desperate moments."

Blake laughed softly. "Just speak from your heart."

"My heart is saying, please don't let me die."

"You nearly had it right. Next time try, please don't let me die, God."

"If we ever get through this, promise me you'll go somewhere with me?"

"Where?"

"I don't care. Movie, restaurant, nightclub. I'd even go to your church with you as long as it wasn't because we were hiding out from a demon. Just somewhere. You and me."

"We'll get through this."

"Blake–"

"Shh, Allie Cat. We'll go out somewhere. Even if it's to Mass to thank God for helping us survive."

"A nightclub would be more fun," Allie suggested.

Blake stilled, his head came up like he listened for something. "Demon's gone."

"How–"

"Like calls to like." He held up his left arm. "Come on. Let's get as close as possible to the meeting point. Keep low."

They had nearly reached the road when Nathan and Eric spotted them. Instead of running towards them, they ran for their car, which was the closest choice. Blake grabbed Alyssa's hand and they ran to the road. He pulled out his phone as they ran.

"Make it quick," Blake said as soon as his call was

answered. He ended the call and tucked the phone in his pocket.

"How far away are they?" Alyssa clutched at her stomach, a stitch starting.

"Seconds."

"They better be." The words were barely out of her mouth when Blake's four-wheel-drive raced around a corner, heading towards them. Alyssa stopped, her hands resting on her knees as she tried to slow her breathing.

Alex pulled up beside them and the back door swung open. Alyssa hopped in as Riley moved out of the way, Blake behind her. Alex took off as soon as the door was closed. Alyssa buckled up as she recalled the first time she'd been in a vehicle Alex drove.

He wove in and out of streets and even though Alyssa watched behind them, she didn't see any sign of Nathan.

When they reached the highway, Alex asked, "Where to?"

"West." Blake answered. "Second exit off the highway."

Alyssa watched out the rear window until they turned off the highway. Even then she regularly had to check they weren't being followed. When she started to turn again, Blake reached out and placed his hand against her face so she couldn't turn.

"Relax, Allie Cat."

"I can't. He wanted to catch us so badly, I could almost taste it." She frowned. "That sounds demented."

"No more than the rest of it. Put your head on my shoulder and sleep. You look wrecked."

"Or there's always my shoulder. I bet it's more comfortable than his." Riley grinned as he patted the spot he offered.

Alyssa smiled slightly. She leaned against Blake, her eyes only half open. "Just for a minute. Then I have to ring Erin." She yawned. Her eyes shut involuntarily. When next she opened them, the vehicle was stopped. She sat up and looked around. Only Blake was in the vehicle with her.

"Hey, sleepyhead."

"Why didn't you wake me? I had to ring Erin."

"Riley rang her."

"How long are we stopping here for?"

"Just long enough to get fuel."

"You weren't going to tell me?"

"We're only going another couple of k's up the road. We'll stop there for breakfast."

"I'll be back in a minute." Alyssa grabbed her

backpack and hopped out. She looked around until she saw a restroom sign and headed for it. By the time she made it back, they were waiting for her. Blake stood by the open door, a cup of coffee in his hands.

"If you'd woken me when you first stopped, I wouldn't have held you up."

"Did you hear anyone complain, Allie Cat?"

"Not yet."

"Did you get out of the wrong side of bed, Allie?" Riley grinned at her as she climbed into the vehicle.

"She's hungry," Alex said.

"Argh." Alyssa stared straight ahead. She wished she sat at a window so she could look out it and pretend none of them existed.

* * *

They stopped again at midday and set up camp at a roadside stop. It was well treed with signs welcoming people to camp for forty-eight hours. Riley had a campfire going and a billy heating while Alex set up the tent. Alyssa helped Scarlett collect firewood. She glanced around and wondered where Blake had disappeared.

"Did you see where Blake went?"

"No."

Alyssa stared at Scarlett. "You don't like me much, do you?"

"It doesn't matter if I do or don't. I have a job to do and I'll do it."

"Why don't you like me?"

"I never said I disliked you."

"Forget it. I'm going to see if I can find Blake." Alyssa turned towards the camp. She spun to face Scarlett when she spoke.

"How many of them do you need dangling after you?" Scarlett's eyes blazed, one hand planted firmly on her hip, the other clutching firewood.

"I don't know what you mean." Alyssa's chin came up, her own anger starting to rise.

"Yeah right! You have my brother following you around like a puppy and now you're stalking my cousin. Leave them alone!"

"Alex?" Her anger evaporated instantly.

"Don't try and tell me you had no idea. You know exactly how appealing you are to males. And you use makeup to improve that appeal. How about you stop throwing yourself at them all the time."

"In case you didn't realise there's a demon after me."

"I don't see you throwing yourself at me."

"With how welcoming you are? I'd probably risk frostbite."

Scarlett momentarily closed her eyes. When she

opened them, they were devoid of emotion. "I refuse to get into a name calling match with you. Fine, you're right, I don't like you, but I will protect you from Retribution. I've sworn an oath to protect humanity from demons and my personal feelings don't come into it. But stay away from Alex and Blake."

"What? No warning me off Riley?"

"He can take care of himself. But you don't kick a man when he's down. So leave the other two alone."

"Or what?"

"No threats. Just leave them alone. They're putting their lives at risk for you. Have the decency not to rip their hearts out while they're at it." Scarlett spun and stalked away.

Alyssa fought the urge to call her back and apologise. I haven't done anything wrong, she told herself. Her gaze was drawn to the campfire Scarlett strode towards. Alex sat by himself and stared into the flames. Riley made himself a cup of tea and Blake was nowhere to be seen.

She made her way over to the fire and dropped the handful of firewood. "Has anyone seen Blake?"

"Yeah, he-" Riley began, only to be cut off by Scarlett's glare.

"Never mind. I'll have a look myself," Alyssa said.

"Allie." Riley put another cup in front of him and started to make a coffee.

"What?"

"You might want to take this to him." He stirred the drink before he handed it to her. "That way." He pointed out the direction and ignored the noise Scarlett made. "Try not to get lost. Four hours and we leave."

Alyssa found Blake sitting on a fallen log. She silently handed him the coffee and sat beside him. Other than a thank you, he remained quiet. Alyssa glanced over at him. He continued to sip his drink and stare in front of him.

Alyssa waved a fly away that tried to settle on her. "What are you doing?"

"Thinking."

"About?" Alyssa had almost given up on an answer, when Blake turned to look at her.

"What do you want me to say, Allie Cat? That I was thinking about you?"

Alyssa ignored the rush of anger his words brought. Instead, she forced a smile to her lips. "Well in that case, were you thinking or fantasising?"

Blake continued to look at her for another minute before his lips curved into a smile. "Allie Cat. What am I going to do with you?" He shook his head slowly.

"I can give you some ideas."

"I'll just bet you can. Behave. Come on, it's probably safer if we went back to the camp, siren."

"I'm not a siren."

"You wouldn't say that if you could see yourself through my eyes."

"Really?"

"No need to look pleased with yourself. I'm an expert at resisting temptation." Alyssa frowned and Blake laughed when he saw it. "Come on, Allie Cat." He held out his hand, which Alyssa willingly took.

Chapter Twenty

Alyssa tucked the card with the Lord's Prayer on it into her book. She only had a few chapters left to read. She stared thoughtfully at the front cover. She tried to stretch, but there wasn't much room when you were pressed between two large males. Alex was on one side of her, sleeping, while Blake was on the other. Scarlett drove and Riley sat in the front passenger seat using the small laptop. Alyssa smiled as she listened to him mutter about poor coverage.

She frowned down at the book and then sighed. The one problem with reading Patrick's book was he expected the reader to have a religious background. She didn't even know the proper name for the wafer. Well, she did now, but only because she'd asked Alex what Patrick was talking about in one of the earlier chapters.

"Spit it out, Allie Cat," Blake said softly.

Startled, she glanced up at him. She looked down at the book and opened to the start of the chapter she'd just read. She handed it to Blake.

After a quick glance, Blake handed the book back to her. "What do you need to know?"

"Is it possible?"

Blake sighed. "Maybe you should be asking a different question."

"Like?"

"Ask yourself if you can face your strongest desires and deny them."

"No!" Scarlett said from the front of the vehicle. "We aren't going to bind the demon."

"Wrong chapter Scarlett. She's thinking of tempting him," Blake said.

"She'll never be able to hold him."

"I think I'm a better judge of that then you, Scarlett." Alyssa fought the anger Scarlett's words called up.

"Okay, then tell me, if you were faced by the one thing you wanted above everything else, would you be able to turn it down. Actually, if you were offered every single thing you ever wanted, would you be able to turn them all down?" Scarlett glanced at her in the rear view mirror.

"Would you be able to, Scarlett?"

Scarlett nodded. "That's part of our training. We get to face a minor demon of temptation. Fail that and you don't become a hunter."

"Allie Cat, we're not talking a minor demon here. His power'll enhance your desires. You could step right out of sanctuary and into his lying arms. He'd give you all you ever wanted. You just wouldn't live long enough to enjoy it for more than a few minutes."

"But if we can stop him from leaving and telling Nathan where we are, the night won't be so difficult."

"She has a point," Riley said.

"Of course she has a point. It doesn't mean she'll be able to cope with it," Scarlett said.

"That'd simplify matters for you then," Alyssa said.

"Enough!" Blake looked between Scarlett and Alyssa. "The discussion is ended until we reach the next sanctuary."

"I–"

"Allie Cat." Blake interrupted her.

Alyssa looked away from him to find Alex was now awake and watching her. She leaned her head back and stared at the roof lining of the vehicle. She only hoped the next stop wasn't too far away. She had to get away from them all for a minute.

It was another half an hour before they pulled up at

a service station in the next town. They refuelled the vehicle, used the restrooms and grabbed some take-away before they piled in the vehicle and drove to the church on the outskirts of the town. It was a small timber church that was nearly a hundred years old.

Scarlet pulled on the park brake. "I'll see the caretaker about the key Uncle Joe arranged for us to have."

"Take Riley and Alex with you," Blake said.

There was a moment of silence where they all stared at each other before silently climbing out of the vehicle to leave Alyssa and Blake alone.

"I hate it when you all do that."

"What, Allie Cat?"

"Like there's a silent conversation happening and I'm not part of it."

"We know each other very well. Too well sometimes. It can be as much of a curse as a blessing."

"Blake, I want to keep Retribution here tonight. Are you going to help me?"

"Straight to the point. That's what I like about you, Allie."

"Are you going to help me?"

"What sort of help are you looking for?"

"I don't know. What sort of help can you give me?"

"Not a great deal. You'll be facing most of it alone.

Physical restraint won't help if you invite the demon to have your soul in exchange for all he promises."

"I've thought about what he could offer."

"And?"

"My strongest desires would be you and Nathan."

"Thanks, Allie Cat," Blake said dryly.

Alyssa smiled. "Nathan's death and you… well, just you."

"No need to spell it out."

"You could help me and then I'd only have one desire to battle."

Blake grinned. "Nice try, Allie Cat."

Alyssa became serious. "How hard is it, Blake?"

He took her hand and held it between both of his. His gaze met hers, all humour gone. "One of the hardest things you'll ever do. Providing the blood'll be the easy part. It's surviving the temptations that'll make you want to fling yourself on the demon's mercy. But they don't have any."

"Will you stay by my side through it?"

Blake closed his eyes for a second. "If you need me to."

"Blake if–"

"I'll stay with you. But don't let me down, Allie Cat. I won't be able to stand by and watch if you give yourself to the demon."

"What happened?" She rested her hand on his demon mark.

Blake shook his head. "Not now. Maybe later. But definitely not tonight. Come on. Looks like they got the key. Let's check our accommodations before it grows dark."

Riley threw the key to Blake once they were out of the vehicle. "It has the same electrical system it had when it was first built nearly a century ago."

Alyssa frowned. "No electricity?"

He held up his other hand to show the four candles he'd been given. He grinned. "Don't look like it's the end of the world."

"I'm beginning to hate the dark." Alyssa glanced over to the last rays of the sun lighting the horizon.

"Give me a minute, Allie Cat. Let me see what the church is like before you make any firm decisions."

Alyssa nodded and watched as Blake walked alone to the church. She turned back to the other three to see Riley and Scarlett nodding to something Alex had said.

"What's going on?" Alyssa asked Alex as Riley and Scarlett moved away.

"Alyssa, we can manage without you risking yourself like this."

"If I can keep the demon here tonight, we can start

heading towards home and find somewhere closer to set up and wait out the month. That's what you really want, isn't it? To let the month pass so those who called him have to deal with him?"

"What I really want is a way to send the demon back to where he came from, but he's too powerful for us to do that. The four of us have no tie to him and no way of gaining one." Alex hesitated. "What if you can't manage to resist temptation?"

"Have some faith in me."

"I thought you don't believe in faith?"

"Then we're screwed, because I'm not sitting around letting you all stand in front of me when I should be in the front line. This is my problem. My mistake. I have to take responsibility for it where I can. If Blake tells me that church over there's a strong sanctuary," she pointed at it, "I'll face the demon tonight."

Alex reached into his backpack and pulled out a knife in an ill-fitting leather sheath. "Then you might like to have this."

Alyssa stared at the knife Nathan had used to make her bleed. She took a step back and looked up at Alex.

"It's yours now. You made it yours when you used it on the demon. And I had Father Joe bless it. It's pure again."

Alyssa hesitantly reached out and took it. She put it in her backpack. "Not quite what I was asking for when I said I wanted a blessed sword, but I guess we're getting closer."

Alex smiled fleetingly. "Just make sure you take care of yourself. Blake isn't the only one who'd be devastated if we were to lose you to the demon."

"Alex, if I had a brother–"

"Please, Alyssa. I'm not dense."

Alyssa felt her cheeks grow hot. "I'm sorry."

"Don't be. Just make sure you survive the night. I don't want to have nightmares similar to Blake's." He shook his head when Alyssa opened her mouth. "And don't ask me about it. It's Blake's story to tell. Besides, I don't know all of it. I arrived too late to help." He looked past Alyssa and she turned to see what captured his attention.

She smiled when she saw Blake walk towards them. He didn't return her smile. That was answer enough for her. And for Alex who placed a hand on her shoulder and clasped it lightly before he moved away to leave them alone.

Blake took both her hands and stared intently at her. "Be very sure, Allie Cat. Some mistakes can never be rectified."

She stared back at him. She thought carefully over all she'd read and all she'd been told. "I'm sure."

"Then I guess we need to do some preparations. Have you got your prayer card?"

Alyssa rolled her eyes. "I wish you'd all stop trying to arm me with a prayer."

Blake shook his head. "You worry me, Allie Cat. A gun might be good against flesh and blood, but a prayer is a dangerous weapon to a demon. Especially the Lord's Prayer since you don't have to believe a single word for it to work."

Chapter Twenty-One

Alyssa stared at the small bowl of blood sitting in the open doorway of the church. The knife lay beside it. Her hand brushed over the new bandaid near the faint pink line from the last cut. She had no idea how she was going to explain them, but they made it look like she had serious issues.

A candle sat on either side of the door and cast leaping shadows around her. She looked up at the stars as they played hide and seek in the clouds, surprised at how normal everything seemed. Crickets chirped in the background, a soft breeze blew away the heat of the day and a few lights dotted the handful of houses that made up the town.

The metallic smell of blood seemed to grow stronger. Alyssa glanced up as Blake came to stand beside her. He sat, the warmth of his body pressed against her right side. He put his arm around her and drew her close. His arm rested along hers where it lay on her drawn up knees. Alyssa could feel the tension in him. She stared at the demon mark on the arm that lay on hers. The smell of blood seemed to fill the air.

"He's close, isn't he?"

Blake's arm tightened on her. "Yes."

Alyssa swallowed, her eyes closing momentarily. "How far away?"

"Minutes." Silence fell between them. "You don't have to go through with this. I can cover the blood and we can join the others near the altar."

Alyssa turned her head. The candle flames caused shadows to leap across Blake's face and twin flames shone in his eyes. "I need to do this. I can do this."

"Make sure you get through this night in one piece. We have a date when all this is over."

Alyssa smiled. "I'll keep that in mind." The smile evaporated as the breeze picked up and the candles leapt high until they thinned to nothingness. The darkness crept in around them. Alyssa reluctantly turned her head to stare into the night. She shuddered as she smelt the scent that haunted her nightmares. The mixture of bushfires, metal and rotten eggs. She couldn't see him clearly. His was a dark shadow amongst the other lighter shadows. And then she could see his eyes. Mesmerising pools of hell.

Alyssa couldn't help the shudder that went through her body.

Blake's arm tightened on her again. "I'm here. You're not alone. No matter what happens, you're not alone."

Alyssa stared into the dark and wondered what would happen. The minutes stretched out and the demon continued to stand in front of her. She began to relax against Blake.

"Stay alert, Allie Cat. Your body's safe in sanctuary as long as he can't invade your mind."

Alyssa sat up straight. She waited. Her mind drifted and she thought of other days. Days of sunshine, beaches, parties, friends. Her eyes closed. She could smell the scent of the ocean, a warm body pressed against hers on the sand. She opened her eyes to see Blake lean in to her and his head blocked the sun from her eyes. He hovered close, just out of reach.

"What do you want, Allie?"

"Blake?"

"Tell me what you want. Only ask and it's yours."

Alyssa looked into his eyes, her mouth opened to tell him. She noticed the glints of black radiating from his pupil to bleed into the blue of his eyes. She trembled. "Blake?"

"Come on, Allie. What do you want from me?"

"Blake... I..." she hesitantly reached up to touch him, but he drew back.

"Come on, Allie. All you have to do is ask. Why won't you ask?"

There was a hard edge to Blake's voice and Alyssa frowned. Playing a hunch, Alyssa tried to bring the words to mind that she needed. "Our Father, who art in heaven, hallowed be thy name. Thy Kingdom come, thy will be done-"

Blake hissed and drew back from her. "What do you think you're doing, Allie?"

Alyssa closed her eyes and tried to think of the next lines. She couldn't. So she started again. "Our Father, who art in heaven-"

"Enough, Allie." Blake shook her and her eyes flew open. "Enough."

The black in his eyes spread until she was looking into dark bottomless pits. "Retribution."

The demon smiled. He still wore Blake's face. "Come on, little Allie Cat. All you have to do is ask."

"And spend eternity in hell?"

"That's only for those who believe in it. Hell is in their mind. Just like heaven. There is no God. Demons don't prove his existence. There's nothing after this life so you'd better enjoy it while you can. What do you want? Ask and it's yours. I'll claim you after you've enjoyed it all. You'll have years to enjoy it. What more could you want, human?"

"I don't believe you."

"We don't break any promise made."

"But you twist them to suit yourselves."

"Set the terms, Allie. That's all you have to do. You set them. I fill them. If you say you wish to live to a hundred, then I'll give it to you. You have to be clear. If you aren't clear I have to fill in the blanks. That's always the problem with you humans. You leave too many blanks to be filled in. You can't complain if we don't always get it right."

Alyssa frowned. "But don't you need a living sacrifice?"

Retribution stared at her out of Blake's face, a smile twisting his lips. "I can wait. I have the patience of centuries. Name your price. Come on, Allie Cat. You have only to ask. I'm here to serve you."

"No one gives something without expecting payment. What's your price?"

"You, love. Just you. But I can wait for you. You can have your life first." He bent close and his breath caressed her lips. "You can have the world. You can hold it in your palm and do with it as you will."

"Me in exchange for the world. As highly as I think

of myself, even I can't see how I can command such a steep price."

"You think too much, Allie. Try feeling instead." Retribution's hand moved slowly from her hip and glided along her side.

Alyssa reached out and grabbed his wrist. She ignored the warmth that flooded her body. "You might wear his face, but it's only a mask. I see the lie in your eyes."

"I can give you the reality. You only have to ask. He'll be your devoted slave for life."

"What about free will?"

"What about it? You want him, don't you?"

"I want him, not the shell of him."

"Then ask me for him."

"You can't give me what I want. Without it being offered of his own free will, it's worthless."

"It will be his free will. I will intensify what's already there."

"No."

"You humans are stubborn creatures. I offer you the world. You dare to throw it back at me? You don't want to do that, Allie."

"Or what? You'll kill me? Isn't that what you plan to do anyway?"

"Maybe you'll change your mind after a taste of the tortures of the damned."

"I won't give in."

"We'll see, little rabbit." Blake's face blurred and became Nathan's. The eyes remained the same.

Alyssa's first instinct was to scream. Instead she closed her eyes. She felt Retribution's hands press against the side of her head. Pain shot through her and she was once again staring into Retribution's eyes.

"You can't escape me. I'm in you. Around you. I am you."

"No."

"Tell me you're mine and I'll set you free."

"No!" Pain shot through her and Alyssa screamed. "No!"

"That's it, scream little rabbit. Scream for me."

"Let me go," Alyssa said through clenched teeth. "I'm not yours. I'll never be yours." She writhed as more pain shot through her. She bit her lip as she tried to hold back the scream. The metallic taste of blood filled her mouth.

Retribution pressed his lips to hers. "If I have to take it one drop at a time I will."

Alyssa turned her head away. "I'm not some dammed cocktail you can sip on when you're thirsty."

The demon's fingers tightened on her head and he turned her back to face him.

"You're mine, Allie. I'll do as I please with you. You have only to claim you're mine and I'll please you instead."

"Never!" She couldn't hold back the scream. Pain shot through her body like fire. Before her eyes Nathan became the demon, his wings furled behind him, the heat of his body burned against hers. She pushed against him, tried to pull away, but he had her pinned, his fingers a brand on either side of her face. "Let me go!"

"I will cherish you, Allie. I'll make you what you are meant to be."

"I'll make myself what I'm meant to be."

"Stubborn child. All you have to do is say 'I am yours. My soul I give to you' and all the pain will vanish. You need never feel another ounce of pain again in your life."

"No!" Alyssa gasped the word out between the waves of pain that wracked her body. "Our Father-"

"Don't go there, Alyssa. You won't like what happens if you go there."

"Who... art in... heaven." Alyssa sobbed the words out, the pain so strong she didn't think she could handle another minute of it. "Hallowed… be… thy name."

"Alyssa!"

She tried to block her ears, the pain of his shriek made her ears feel like they must bleed at the sound. "Thy…. Kingdom… come." Alyssa felt her body being lifted from the sand and flung from the demon. Then he was standing over her and the beach was no more. A desert like place that had a red haze to it swam before her eyes. "Thy will… be done."

"You don't believe in him. Why call on one you don't believe in?"

"On earth… as it is… in… heaven." Alyssa struggled to her feet. She reached out to steady herself on a boulder. "I don't believe in you either. And yet here you are." She swayed on her feet, the pain not as strong as it had been a moment ago. "But I guess it doesn't matter if I believe in God or not. Apparently he believes in me." She grinned, "And you believe in him, or this prayer wouldn't work."

"You'll pay dearly for this." The demon was in front of her. He reached out with one hand and grasped her throat. "Say you're mine and you can live."

Alyssa felt the air catch in her throat, but she

ploughed on, her voice a whisper. "Give us this day… our daily bread."

"This will be your last day."

"And forgive us our trespasses." Alyssa breathed easier as the grip on her throat eased. She stood a little straighter.

"Stop!"

"As we forgive those who trespass against us." The hand fell from her throat. "And lead us not into temptation."

"Alyssa, how can you treat me like this?" The demon became Blake. "I give you my love and you treat me like this."

Alyssa focused on the eyes. The twin pools of hell. "But deliver us from evil. For thine is the kingdom, the power and the glory, for ever and ever." The demon wavered before her eyes. Alyssa's grin widened. "Amen." Everything went black, spiralling into a lengthy nothingness.

"Allie Cat. Talk to me."

Alyssa tried to open her eyes, but it seemed impossible. She could feel hard floorboards under her. She opened her mouth to speak, but no words came to mind. Then she was being lifted and cradled against a warm chest. She breathed in, and could smell only Blake. There was no scent of bushfires, metal and rotten eggs. She struggled to sit up properly and her eyes flickered open. She squinted, the light from the lantern someone had placed nearby seemed too bright.

"Shh, Allie Cat. An hour till dawn. He's gone for now. The coming light would've helped, but you did it. You resisted temptation. Nathan hasn't the time to find us before we can move on."

Alyssa sagged against Blake's chest and her body started to tremble. So close to dawn? It hadn't felt like hours. How had so much time passed? She felt someone lift her hand and press a warm mug into it. She turned and was surprised to see it was Scarlett.

"It's sweet tea. Drink it," Scarlett said.

Blake had to steady her hand so she could take a sip. The warmth hit her stomach and made her realise how cold she was. She watched as Scarlett draped a blanket over her. She frowned and breathed in deep. She could only smell the scent of Blake and sweet tea. She stared at Scarlett.

Scarlett met her stare with one of her own. Then she smiled. "Sorry I was so hard on you. I guess you did have what it takes to resist temptation."

"I was prepared." Alyssa frowned at how raspy her voice sounded.

Scarlett chuckled. "It's a good thing the caretaker is

as deaf as a doorpost. With how loud you screamed he'd have been over here demanding what was going on if he'd heard."

"I screamed?"

"And recited the Lord's Prayer. I was surprised you made it all the way through," Scarlett said.

"So was I. I just kept picturing the prayer card. I've seen it enough times since I've been using it as a bookmark. And read it a few times. I can't," Alyssa swallowed. "I can't believe it worked."

Alex came to squat beside her. "We told you it was a better weapon than a gun against demons."

"But I don't believe in him."

"You already answered that question once tonight, Allie Cat."

Alyssa groaned and momentarily closed her eyes. "Did I say it all out loud?" She tried desperately to remember every word she'd spoken. The only thing she could recall clearly was the pain.

Riley put his hands on Scarlett and Alex's shoulders. "We'll give you some space, Allie."

"Here." Scarlett held a tissue out to her. When Alyssa frowned, Scarlett touched her own lips. "For the blood."

Alyssa took the tissue and dabbed at her lip as the three demon hunters retreated. Alyssa took a deep breath. "You said the demon gains power from consuming my blood."

"He'd have gained power tonight, Allie Cat."

"I didn't even finish asking my question."

"It wasn't hard to figure out your question. Especially since after your lip started to bleed you told him you weren't a cocktail."

"What else did I say?"

"Nothing I don't already know."

Alyssa met his gaze. "What did I say?"

"That you want me," Blake said softly.

"Was that all?"

"That you want me of my own free will. Not a shell of me."

"He offered to make you my devoted slave. To let me live till I was a hundred and give me the whole world to do with as I wanted."

"What made you say no?"

"I want you, not some imitation of you."

"And the world? Why did you turn down the world?"

"I've grown up in a very cynical household. If it looks or sounds too good to be true, then it probably is." Alyssa took another mouthful of tea and made a face. "Please tell me I don't have to drink this. There's too much sugar in it."

Blake's lips slowly curved into a smile. "No, Allie Cat." He put the mug near the lantern.

Alyssa frowned. "Are you okay?"

Blake nodded.

"What's wrong?"

Blake's arms tightened around her. "I could only listen. Listen and hold you. And wait. It's been a long night, Allie Cat."

"How many more nights have we got?"

"Not again. You don't have to go through this again. Each night'll be more difficult."

"How many nights until the month is up, Blake?"

Instead of answering, Blake lifted her left hand and turned it so she could see the pulse at her wrist. There was a demon mark one centimetre in length. Alyssa looked uncertainly from her wrist to Blake.

"Welcome to the club, Allie Cat."

"But… I…why?"

"Your body might have been in sanctuary, but your soul was out there with him. Don't do it again, Allie Cat. Please."

"I have to do something. I can't sit by and let him bring Nathan to us each night. One of us will end up getting shot." At the sound of footsteps, Alyssa looked over Blake's shoulder to see Scarlett walk towards them.

Scarlett picked up the lantern and the mug. "Time to move out." She looked from one to the other for a moment before she turned and walked back to Riley and Alex.

Alyssa tried to rise to her feet, but her body was exhausted and wouldn't cooperate. Blake stood and helped her stand. He guided her to the front passenger seat of his vehicle and pulled the visor down to reveal a mirror.

"Have a look, Allie." He pulled the hair away from her temple and Alyssa adjusted the visor so she could see. The skin was slightly blistered. She turned her head and pulled her hair back from the other side of her face.

She turned to Blake. "He had his fingers there."

Blake had to lean forward to hear her words. "Are you listening to what you're saying? He can harm you, my Allie Cat." Blake rested his fingers where Retribution had clamped his. "Don't give him another chance."

Alyssa closed her eyes. She couldn't watch him a second longer without giving in to the plea and pain she saw in his eyes. She felt his lips meet hers and she hungrily kissed him back, her hands encircling his neck. Heat raced through her veins and pooled in her stomach. She pressed herself close.

"Allie Cat," Blake murmured. "We have to stop."

"Later." She moved forward the fraction that separated their lips. She gave herself over to sensation and was startled when Blake's hands moved to her arms and untangled them from around his neck. When she frowned, Blake smiled slightly and glanced to his left. Alyssa looked over to see Riley stride towards the vehicle. She turned back to Blake, closed her eyes and dropped her forehead to his chest.

Blake lifted her head with a finger under her chin. "What's wrong?"

"I hope your brother and cousins aren't going with us on our first date."

Blake stared at her for a few seconds before he began to laugh. "Don't pull away, Allie. I wasn't laughing at you. Well, not exactly. I guess I'm relieved to see you being… you. Come on. Let's get in the vehicle. I'd say Scarlett and Alex have already locked up and returned the key." Blake took her arm and guided her to the back door.

Alyssa shook her head. "You hop in first. I want the window seat." She ignored his knowing smile.

Chapter Twenty-Two

Alyssa sat on one of the camp chairs next to Scarlett while Riley and Blake changed a rear tyre. Alex was at the front of the vehicle with the small laptop perched on the bonnet. He glanced at his watch and then at the laptop. Alyssa closed her eyes. She didn't want to see what was happening. They'd driven west most of the day so as to put plenty of distance between the church and themselves. They'd taken turns at driving and sleeping in the vehicle. None of them felt rested.

"What I'd really like to do is go to the nearest motel with a large bathtub and soak in it until my skin wrinkles," Alyssa said.

"Mmm. Sounds good." Scarlett waved at the flies that hung around.

"At the moment, even a shower would be good. I feel like I sweated every litre of liquid out of me when we stopped to get the first flat tire fixed." Alyssa opened her eyes, yelping as water was sprinkled on her. She glared at Riley who grinned, a bottle of water in his hands.

"Feel any better?"

Alyssa wiped the droplets of water and sweat from her face. "No, but when I get the energy to move, I'm going to tip that bottle over you."

"Come on, Riley. Give me a hand to get the tyre back under everything," Blake snapped.

Alex walked towards them, the laptop closed and tucked under his arm. "No need to rush. Even if we left this very second and sped the whole way, we'd be about half an hour too late."

Alyssa leapt to her feet. "What are you talking about, Alex?"

"We can't make it to sanctuary in time."

"No! I don't want to hear that. We'll have to drive faster. I'll drive." Alyssa walked towards the driver's seat.

Blake grabbed her by the arm before she reached it. "Allie Cat-"

"No! I don't want to hear it. We will make it to sanctuary."

Alex came to stand beside them. "There's a rest area

about three quarters of an hour from here. We can make a stand there."

Alyssa stared at him. "Stand?"

"We won't leave you unprotected."

"Alex." At Blake's tone Alex nodded and moved away from them to help pack everything in the vehicle. "Walk with me, Allie Cat."

Alyssa shook her head, but allowed Blake to take her hand and walked beside him on the narrow road. They walked in silence and Alyssa had begun to think they'd continue to do so when Blake stopped and faced her.

"You won't tempt him tonight. You'll make a circle with the salt and you'll pray all night. We'll stand between you and the demon."

"You'll get in the circle with me?"

Blake shook his head.

"What aren't you telling me, Blake?"

"You need more than just the circle to keep him out. His tie to you strengthens." Blake touched her wrist. "And his power increases."

Alyssa raised her hands and placed them on Blake's chest. She felt his heart beat beneath her palm. Her gaze clashed with his. "What are our chances of surviving tonight?" When Blake continued to watch her without answering, she turned away. "That's what I thought." She started to walk off, but Blake gripped her shoulders and pulled her back against him. He wrapped his arms about her and rested his chin on her head.

"You will survive the night."

"How?"

"I'll make sure of it."

Alyssa froze, her breath caught in her throat. She tried to turn and face him, but his arms tightened around her. "Tell me you're not going to do what I think you're going to do."

"Is that what you want to hear?"

"Blake! Let me go!" Alyssa pulled away from him and took two steps back. "You won't exchange yourself for me. Promise me you won't."

"I won't watch you die. I can't go through that again."

"I'm not going to watch you die either. Promise me!"

"Allie Cat–"

"Promise me!"

Blake shook his head.

"Then I'll offer myself to him the moment he arrives. I won't have you dying for me. Do you hear me? What makes you think I want to see someone I care about die anymore than you do?"

Blake reached out to her, "Allie Cat–"

Alyssa stepped back again and shook her head. "No!"

Blake rubbed his palm against his forehead. "Be reasonable."

"You be reasonable. What makes you think my life is more valuable than yours?"

Instead of answering, Blake pulled Alyssa against him. "Shh, Allie Cat."

"Promise me?" She sniffed.

"I promise. But you have to promise to hold out tonight. Fight him. Don't let him take you. Promise?"

"I promise." Alyssa lifted her head off his chest and smiled at him weakly. "I don't suppose I can convince you to join me in celebrating life before we face death?"

Blake chuckled. "Nice try, siren." He dropped a kiss on her forehead.

Alyssa looked up at him through her eyelashes. "Is that the best you can do?"

"Not at all." He continued to smile down at her. "But it's the best you're getting for the moment."

"Hmph." Alyssa started to turn away, but Blake pulled her back into his arms, his lips a breath away from hers.

"Get through the night and I'll show you better." He pulled back as she moved forward, smiling.

"Deal."

Blake glanced up the road to where his family sat waiting in the vehicle. He waved them forward and they stood in the middle of the road, watching the vehicle drive towards them. Once again Alyssa took the window seat.

The rest stop was only thirty-five minutes away. Alex ignored the speed limit in favour of having more time to prepare. He parked the vehicle at the edge of the rest area, where it was nearly surrounded by trees. Then he and Scarlett walked the rest area and removed any large, loose objects.

Riley pulled out the table and chairs while Blake set up the camp stove. Knowing the drill, Alyssa looked through the tinned food and pulled out several tins of the same flavour stew. Riley handed her a saucepan. Within minutes dinner was warming and Alyssa sat in a camp chair, watching as Riley held a mirror for Blake while he shaved.

He'd removed his shirt and Alyssa watched the muscles move under his skin as he ran the razor over his face. When they stopped moving, she looked up to find his gaze on her. She grinned at him. He shook his head, but she was sure he was trying not to smile as he finished shaving. As soon as he'd finished, he swapped places with Riley. Alyssa checked dinner. Finding it hot enough, she ladled it into their shallow bowls and put a loaf of bread and a tin of butter on the table.

She stared at the table. It all looked ordinary. The four original camp chairs, and a folding stool they'd bought at a service station along the way, sat around the table. Thin lines of steam hovered above the bowls of stew and cutlery sat at each place. Ordinary. It was far too mundane to possibly be a last supper.

Scarlett was the first to join her, a brief touch on her shoulder. "Thanks."

Alex sat across from Alyssa and pulled some bread out of the bag and placed it by his bowl. Riley and Blake came to the table, both with shirts on again. Once they were all seated, Riley said grace and Alyssa bowed her head too. She watched as they ate and wondered how they could be so calm.

Blake placed his hand over hers where it rested on her lap. Gazes collided. "Eat up, Allie Cat. You'll need your strength for tonight."

"Oh, no," Scarlett said.

Alyssa turned to see what had caught Scarlett's attention and watched as a vehicle pulled into the rest area.

Riley rose from the table. "I've got it. Who wants to come?" When both Alex and Scarlett rose to their feet he laughed. "The more the merrier. Let's take it slow. Give them a few minutes to use the restroom before we chase them away."

"How will he convince them to leave?" Alyssa asked.

Blake shrugged. "He'll figure it out. Now eat up, Allie Cat."

Alyssa stared up at him. She reached out and ran her hand over his smooth cheek. It was the first time he'd shaved since she'd met him. She couldn't decide if she liked the scruffy look or the clean- shaven look best. Both suited him in her opinion. Blake pulled her hand away to drop a kiss in her palm. Then he closed his hand over hers so her hand closed too.

"Eat, Allie Cat."

Alyssa held his gaze a moment longer before she turned to her food, the feel of his lips imprinted on her palm.

Alyssa had nearly finished dinner when Riley, Scarlett and Alex arrived back at the table with Scarlett scolding Riley.

"Pride is a sin, Riley."

"But you must admit I got them moving." Riley sat

at the table again. "And I don't think you should be lecturing me on pride."

Scarlett glanced at Alyssa. "I have trouble admitting I'm wrong. That's different."

Riley grinned and glanced first at Alyssa and then at Alex. "Unlike Sir Perfect over there."

Alyssa's jaw dropped. "Oh, you didn't." She dropped her head into her hands.

Blake pulled her hands from her face. "We share everything."

"Why?"

"If we've done nothing to be ashamed of then there's no reason we can't share everything, is there?"

"But-" she glanced towards Alex, then back at Blake. "Every little thing?"

Blake smiled wryly. "Almost. Some things are too traumatic to share with anyone but our priest."

"But… I mean… what about…"

Blake took pity on her, "Some questions family'll never ask." He turned to Riley. "You want to tell us how you managed to shift the visitors on so quickly?"

Alyssa turned to Riley, trying to ignore the heat in her cheeks. She busied herself eating the rest of her meal.

Riley grinned. "I invited them to our dusk to dawn

prayers. And told them we wouldn't be the only ones attending."

Alyssa grinned. Not so long ago she'd have disappeared quickly too. She finished her last mouthful of dinner and handed her bowl to Blake, who gathered the dishes. She rose and folded her chair up, putting it away. Within minutes they had everything packed and Riley gathered firewood while Alex shaved with Scarlett holding the mirror for him.

Alyssa stayed at Blake's side. If this might be their last day, she wanted to spend every second with him. She thought of Erin and wished she'd known when she rang her earlier that this might be her final hours. Then she was relieved she hadn't. She was glad their last conversation had been upbeat. And she'd even managed a phone call to her mother without arguments. That should've given her a warning her world was about to end.

"You want me to roll the swag out for you? There's at least an hour before he gets here." Blake caught her lock of crimson hair in his fingers. He let it spill out to fall amongst the darker strands.

Alyssa caught his hand as he was about to pick it up again. "I don't think I could sleep."

"I'll roll it out and you can rest then."

Alyssa shook her head and her fingers tightened on his hand.

"I'll stay with you."

"Okay then."

"Dangerous situations create strong, but temporary attachments between people."

"If we survive this, you'll soon find returning to a normal life won't change my feelings. The only thing the situation has made different is how fast I moved." She grinned. "Not that I normally have much patience with starting off slow."

Blake stared at her for a few seconds before he nodded. "I'll get the swag."

Alyssa watched him as he pulled the swag out of the vehicle and rolled it out on a grassy spot. Alyssa joined him and sat on the edge of the swag. "You'll stay with me?"

Blake nodded. "Yes."

Alyssa lay on her side and looked up at him. "There's plenty of space beside me." She laughed at his expression. "No attempt to try and change your mind. You look tired."

Blake stared at her, finally nodding. She watched as he lay on his side behind her. They both barely fit together on the swag. He tucked an arm under his head, the other he draped over her hip.

Alyssa lay her head down and closed her eyes. She sank against his warmth and drifted off only to be startled awake an hour later as Blake whispered her name in her ear. She stretched and turned her head to look at him. It was too dark to see more than shadows.

"Did you get any sleep, Blake?"

"Yeah."

"Good." She reached out to touch his arm and quickly drew back from the heat of him. "Blake?"

"He's close. Maybe ten minutes."

Alyssa reached out to his arm again. This time when she felt the heat, she wrapped her fingers around it. "Your mark."

Blake took her hand in his right hand. "Like calls to like. He's growing in power, Allie Cat. Even a week might be too long. I'm guessing Nathan's giving him some of his own blood in exchange for telling him where we are."

"Can he do that?"

"Does he strike you as the sort of person who'll be deterred by pain?"

"No."

"It won't give him the same strength of power as yours, but every degree Retribution's power increases, the harder he'll be to fight."

"Why won't his blood give him the same power as mine? Isn't blood… well, blood?"

"No. It's more to do with the agreement struck than the type of blood. Your blood called him forth and sealed the bargain. Your blood is what he needs to complete the bargain with the most power for him." Blake rose to his feet and held out his hand to help her up. "Time to prepare."

Chapter Twenty-Three

Alyssa let him draw her to her feet. He held her hand longer than needed before he let it go to roll up the swag. Alyssa followed him to the vehicle. She took out her knife and prayer card. Blake handed her a jar of salt and a vial of holy water then slung his sword on his back.

"Blake, how do you manage to carry that sword everywhere? I mean, haven't you ever had police question you or one of the family for carrying a sword around?"

"I carry a card saying I'm a member of a living history group. If the police ever query us, we tell them we're on the way to a training session."

"I thought you were against lying."

"We make sure it isn't a lie. Come on, Allie Cat. He's nearly here."

Alyssa walked with Blake to the fire. She quickly

made a circle around herself with salt and the holy water. She checked the prayer card was in the back pocket of her jeans then looked at each of the demon hunters in turn. Their faces were solemn as they bowed their heads in prayer.

Alyssa waited until they crossed themselves and drew their swords before she spoke. "I need you all to promise me something." When they remained silent, she continued. "None of you are to offer yourselves in exchange for my life."

"Fair enough." Riley glanced towards Alex. "I certainly don't have a hero complex."

"I want the words, Riley. They start with I promise."

Riley grinned. "I promise not to offer myself as a sacrifice in exchange for the demon to leave you live out your natural life without any demonic interference."

"Please tell me you weren't thinking of it. Those words sounded extremely well planned."

Riley shook his head. "Just part of the training. Learning how to word things when talking to demons. Although we do try and avoid talking to demons whenever possible."

Alyssa turned to Scarlett.

"I promise the same as Riley."

"We're running out of time, Allie Cat."

"Alex. You have to promise or I'm stepping out of this circle."

"Allie Cat–"

"Stay out of this, Blake."

"Alyssa, I promised you–"

Alyssa cut Alex off. "Now."

"I promise the same as Riley."

"Thank you." Alyssa relaxed. She watched as they turned their backs to her. Each one faced a different direction. The wind picked up and they spread their feet to maintain their balance.

"Pray, Allie Cat," Blake ordered as the demon appeared before them.

Alyssa began the Lord's Prayer, her gaze drawn to the demon that paced outside the circle of swords. She turned so she could continue to face him. There was no way she could have her back to him and wondered how the demon hunters could bring themselves to stay in position when he walked to the other side of the circle.

"Come out and play, little rabbit. What are you doing hiding in there?" Retribution called.

Alyssa continued to pray, staring at the demon while avoiding his eyes. She tried to hold the fear back, but she couldn't stop wondering how they'd make it through the night.

"I can feel Nathan call me, little rabbit. He wants to know where you are. He's willing to offer blood for what he wants. Why aren't you?"

Alyssa couldn't think what came next in the prayer. All she could focus on was the demon bringing Nathan to them. "I thought you were more powerful than that."

Retribution continued to stare at her. "Better than you have tried to play word games with me, rabbit, cat, or whatever name they call you by. You can't beat me."

"Pray, Allie Cat. Don't talk to him."

"Listen to the human, Allie. You can't win against me."

Alyssa's chin rose. "When you go running at the call of a mere human, what can I think?"

"That is where you're wrong. I am here while he's called me a dozen times at least."

"He's only here because of his tie to you, Allie," Scarlett said. "Otherwise, in this realm, he's at the mercy of the one who's called him. But he chose to answer the first call."

"Why? If you're so powerful, why place yourself under the control of another?" Alyssa asked.

"When someone sends me an invite to dine, I sometimes join the party. But it's my choice. They do not coerce me. Do you know how many living sacrifices are offered these days? Not as many as there used to be. Too many offer an animal. Only the minor ones are desperate enough to fall for that."

"It looks like you didn't do too well in your choice of dinner invites," Alyssa said.

"Allie Cat! What are you trying to do? Stop talking to him."

Retribution laughed and the sound caused a shiver of fear to course through Alyssa. "Dinner might be served late, but I shall dine. And then those who've stood in my way will pay once my power's been brought into this world. Step out here Allie, take my hand and come willingly and I'll forgive your companions. Don't they believe in that? Forgive? Turn the other cheek? Get stomped into the ground a little harder?"

"Allie Cat, please!"

Alyssa ignored Blake. "Your words are as slippery as a pit of snakes. I'd trust the words Nathan speaks before I trust yours. You're pathetic."

"Allie Cat! Enough! Leopard rug!"

"Looks like the big, powerful demon has his hands

tied," Alyssa said when Retribution paced outside the circle.

Blake started to turn towards Alyssa. "Allie-"

Scarlett interrupted him. "Stand your ground, Blake. Don't you dare break formation."

Retribution pointed at Alyssa. "You'll soon cower when I let the other human know where you are."

Fear exploded in her. They couldn't face them both. She pulled her knife from its sheath and dropped the leather to the ground. She hoped the hunters were right and the demon couldn't get past them. She held the blade against her skin and hesitated. A deep breath and she slid the sharp metal across the inside of her arm, hissing at the pain. A line of blood dotted her skin.

She raised her arm. "This what you're waiting for? Then try and get it. It's mine and I refuse to share." She felt blood trickle down her arm and she hoped she hadn't cut too deep.

Retribution roared, flinging himself forward. It was like he hit a clear wall and bounced back. He lifted his arms high and with another roar, wind poured around him and pressed against the circle. "You'll die slow and painful. You'll scream for mercy and I will have none. You've rejected your last chance."

"I didn't reject anything. You chose to see it that way. I threw down a challenge and you lost." Alyssa grinned. Fear raced through her, but she wasn't going to grovel at his feet.

"Challenge! You want to challenge me? Come out here and do it."

"What's wrong? Why can't you come in here?" Alyssa ignored Blake's groan.

Retribution roared and doubled in size to tower over them. He raised his arms and a high keening sound issued from his mouth. The wind began to tear around them. Dust swirled. They had to squint to keep the grit from their eyes. The rest of the world disappeared outside the churning, dust filled winds. An eerie red light seemed to emanate through the dust.

"Now'd be a really good time to start praying, Allie Cat."

"Our Father, who art in heaven," Alyssa began as the wind swirled around them and tore at their bodies with stinging hands.

Before Alyssa had reached the end of the prayer, the night was filled with images of people Alyssa cared for. She could only watch as the images were torn to pieces by the wind, the red light making everything look bloodstained. Alyssa reached out to touch Blake's back as she saw the flesh stripped from his body in the vision on the wind. At the last second she pulled her hand back, remembering to stay in the circle. She began the prayer again. She stood straight, her voice strong.

Several hours later, Alyssa trembled from the effort of staying on her feet in the turbulent winds. Her voice grew hoarse from constantly reciting the Lord's Prayer and her limbs stung from dirt peppering them. Her voice faltered as she watched Erin's face being torn apart.

"Close your eyes, Allie Cat."

"Give me a hot stick. I never want to be able to see again," Alyssa moaned. She clapped her hands over her ears to try and block the sobbing the demon filled the air with.

"Pray, Alyssa," Alex said.

"Pray! I can't think of another bloody word."

"Alyssa!" Scarlett started to turn towards her before she recalled herself and stared straight ahead.

Alyssa started to laugh. She sank to her knees, unable to stand any longer.

Without looking at her, Blake ordered. "Get on your feet, Alyssa. Now!"

Alyssa struggled to her feet. "Stop ordering me around all the time!"

"You're the one who started this challenge. Are you going to give in now?" Blake demanded.

"What about your prayer card?" Alex asked.

"Get it out and start reading, Allie Cat. Now!"

"I hate you," Alyssa muttered at Blake.

"No you don't. So stop sulking."

"Hmph." Alyssa pulled the card from her pocket and started to read from it, the red light bright enough to see the words. She read until her hoarse voice was little more than a whisper. She kept her gaze on the card, unable to watch any more horrors in the winds. It was bad enough listening to them. She swayed on her feet and staggered a few times. She managed to catch herself before she fell. The wind continued to pull, tug and sting. She could no longer think. It was all she could do to read the words on the card. Words that no longer made sense. She was so focused on the card she barely noticed the light illuminating the card had become the first rays of sunlight. Her body swayed so much from exhaustion it took her minutes to realise the winds had died down.

Blake sheathed his sword and wrapped his arms around her. "That's enough, Allie Cat. It's over for now."

She buried her head against his shoulder. Her arms

went around his waist, the fingers of her right hand locked on the card. "I can't go through that again."

"Shh."

"I–"

"Hush, my Allie Cat. We'll worry about it later."

"I have to sit down." When Blake tried to tug her towards the vehicle, she shook her head. "Here. In the dirt."

Blake sat with her. Her head rested on his chest, his chin on her head. Both closed their eyes. Fatigue dragged at their limbs. Scarlett dropped to the ground close to them and leaned against Blake, back to back. Riley lay flat on the ground, his arm shielding his eyes from the light that rapidly filled the sky. Alex forced his shaky legs to carry him to the vehicle. When he staggered back to his companions he carried two bottles of water.

Alex dropped to the ground awkwardly. "Alyssa. Water." He offered one of the bottles to her.

Alyssa turned enough to take the bottle, the card falling from her fingers. She tried to open the lid and failed. Instead, she put the lid in her mouth and clamped it with her teeth so she could use both hands to turn the bottle. She dropped the lid and drank before she handed the bottle to Blake.

"Please tell me we don't have to move from here," Alyssa whispered.

"As soon as we can, we should move closer to the vehicle. We'll need the shade as the sun rises higher," Blake said.

Alyssa groaned. "Can't." She looked at the prayer card sitting in the dirt and picked it up. She didn't bother to dust it before she slipped it in her pocket. She was covered in dirt. A little more wouldn't matter.

"Help me up, Alex." Scarlett handed the water bottle to Riley and held her hand out to her brother.

Alex laughed weakly. "You're going to have to crawl. I couldn't help a flea."

Scarlett got to her knees and crawled to her brother, using him to push herself up. Once she was standing, she held out her hand to him. He gripped her hand and staggered to his feet.

Riley held up his hand, stretched out on the ground, his sword beside him. "Me."

Scarlett and Alex leaned against each other and stared at him. "He's an awful long way from us," Scarlett said.

"He looks pretty comfortable to me," Alex agreed.

"When I find my strength again, you two will pay," Riley warned.

"You need to learn to forgive, Riley," Alex said.

"Yep, I will. Right after I finish paying you two back."

Alyssa smiled. She pulled back far enough so she could meet Blake's gaze. "We survived."

"Barely."

"And it's morning."

"Allie Cat, my brain leaked out my ears some time during the night. If you're trying to make a point, be a little less cryptic."

"I got through the night. I believe you said something about showing me your best."

Blake grinned. "Allie Cat. Don't change, sweetheart." He brushed her hair back from her face.

Alyssa's eyes widened as she saw his demon mark. The tattoo barbs were now crimson. "Blake-"

"Shh, Allie Cat. Everything'll be fine."

"No! You didn't want to fight demons any more. And I forced you into it."

Blake shook his head. "No, you didn't. You made me face personal demons. It was way past time I stopped hiding from them. Thank you."

"But-"

"Come on, Allie Cat. Let's find somewhere more comfortable to collapse." Blake got to his knees. He saw her knife and sheath on the ground in front of them. He picked them up and handed them back to her. He continued to hold them as she tried to take them. Their gazes met and held. "Try not to jump head first into danger all the time."

"I couldn't think of anything else to do. I had to stop him from bringing Nathan."

"Tonight we'll be in sanctuary," Blake said firmly.

Alyssa groaned. "I hope so. I don't think I can do that again. I didn't realise it'd be so difficult."

Blake staggered to his feet and pulled Alyssa up. He reached over and helped Riley and the three of them walked back to the vehicle, Blake in the middle, an arm around Riley and Alyssa's shoulders. They had an arm around his waist to help support each other. Alex and Scarlett followed in similar fashion.

Chapter Twenty-Four

Alyssa opened her eyes, her mouth so dry her lips were starting to crack. She tried to roll over, but couldn't move. She started to panic as her eyes tried to focus, then realised it was Blake's arm around her waist that held her captive. She turned to face him.

"You awake, Blake?"

"Trying not to be." Blake didn't open his eyes.

Alyssa smiled slightly. "I've got to get up."

"Hmmm." Blake pulled her close and his hand lazily glided across her back.

"Any other time and I'd encourage this, but I've really got to get up."

"Huh?" Blake opened an eye slightly.

"Are you awake now?" Alyssa sighed when Blake's hand stilled. "I guess so."

"What's wrong, Allie Cat?"

"I'm trying to get up and you won't let me."

Blake stretched and groaned. Alyssa stood up and stumbled as she tried to keep her balance.

Riley rolled to his side and raised himself up on one arm. "As hard as the ground is to sleep on, I'd like some peace so I can have at least another hour."

Alex yawned, sat up and glanced at his watch. "Can't. Midday. Need to get on the road soon. The alarm would have gone off shortly anyway."

Scarlett rubbed her eyes and sat up. "Wait for me, Allie. Better yet, give me a hand."

Alyssa, who'd started to turn in the direction of the restroom, walked over to Scarlett and held out her hand. "I'm just as likely to fall on top of you."

"I'll take my chances." Scarlett clasped Alyssa's hand and was soon on her feet. "I feel like every inch of my body's coated in dirt."

"Tell me about it," Alyssa muttered.

They were back on the road by two o'clock. Alex had hung blankets in the trees to make a shower room and Riley had heated water while the other three prepared lunch. The wash was basic at best and their first stop when they reached the next town was a motel room where they could shower. The second stop was a Laundromat followed by a drive out to the old cemetery that was no longer in use. The town had grown away from the cemetery, leaving open bushland around it.

Alyssa closed her book as they arrived. She had no need for a bookmark. She stared at the cover, a frown marring her forehead. She tapped the book on her knee.

Blake held the door open. "Are you getting out, Allie Cat?" His gaze was drawn to the book in her hand. "No."

"You don't even know what I'm thinking about."

Blake smiled wryly. "Final chapter?"

Alyssa sighed.

Blake chuckled. "Come here, Allie Cat."

Alyssa slid across the seat and turned to face him. He rested his hands on her shoulders. "We can't keep this up, Blake."

He drew Alyssa forward so he could wrap his arms around her. "I know. But there's no guarantee you'll survive that option."

"Life doesn't come with guarantees. And the longer we wait, the less chance there is it'll work."

"Allie Cat-"

"I don't want to talk about it. Besides, you haven't shown me your best. I'm beginning to think you're all talk."

"Really?"

Alyssa's lips curved slightly. "You wouldn't be trying to wriggle out now, would you?"

"I'm sure you'd never let me."

"Well? I'm waiting. I must say that so far I'd have to rate you pretty low on a scale of one to ten."

Blake pulled her forward until she slid off the seat to stand in front of him. He left one hand at her waist, the other travelled up her back to rest at the nape of her neck. Their gazes met and held. Blake slowly lowered his face closer to hers and stopped millimetres away. "How low, Allie Cat?"

Alyssa's smile had vanished, her lips were parted and she stared up at him. "Really low," she whispered.

"Lying is a sin, Allie Cat."

"You sure I'm lying?"

"Definitely. Your heart rate is faster, your breathing shallow and your pulse erratic. So I'd have to say that really low, should be at least an eight."

"Hmmm. I've been told pride is a sin."

"Statement of fact, Allie Cat."

"And that's all I've heard. Statements. You're all talk, Blake."

"And you've no patience." He brushed his lips across hers and her eyes closed as her pulse leapt and sped up. Blake deepened the kiss before he gradually pulled back.

Alyssa's eyes slowly opened and her lips curved into a smile. "Maybe an eight. I'd have to do more research to be certain."

"You're incorrigible."

Alyssa grinned. "And your ego's already inflated too much to give you a better rating."

"I'm sure I could change your mind."

"That'd entail action rather than talk. I'm not sure you can manage that."

"You're probably right. You're far too tempting." Blake gave her a swift kiss before he stepped away from her. "And you're not to even think about the final chapter."

Alyssa watched as Blake strode to Alex's side. She guessed he was telling Alex about her plans. She looked around and spotted Riley and Scarlett together. She walked towards them, determined to gain support for her plan.

Blake was the hardest one to convince her plan was the only sensible one. Even Alex agreed it was best to try now while she had the strength to win. And when it was time for him to leave her at the edge of the sanctuary to face Retribution alone, Alyssa thought he might change his mind again.

"You only have to call and I'll be there. Make sure you call if you need me, Allie Cat. Sometimes you have to let go of your independence and let others help you."

Alyssa reached up to run her hand over his jaw. Her thumb brushed across his lips when she reached his chin. "I can do this."

He pressed a kiss against her thumb. "I know you can. You're strong in here where it counts." Blake rested his hand over her heart. "But sometimes you need extra strength. I'm here, waiting for you."

"Thank you," Allie said softly.

"Just make sure you remember you have to mingle both your blood and the demon's to bind him to you so you can make him vulnerable. It's not enough just to draw blood from each of you."

Alyssa nodded. "I know." She swallowed hard as she thought of what that would involve.

Blake stared at her a moment longer before he turned and started to walk away.

"Blake." He turned at her call. She stared at him, the words harder than she thought it possible for them to be. "I… wait for me."

"Always."

She frowned as she watched him walk away and wished she could've spoken the three words that were caught in her throat. Instead, she turned to face the night and waited, hands behind her back. She knew the wait wouldn't be long. In fact, they'd expected Retribution twenty minutes ago. But she could feel him coming closer now.

Then he was before her. Barely an arm's length away. But she didn't reach out to touch him. She wasn't crazy. Not yet, anyway.

"You waiting for me, human?"

"I was beginning to think you weren't going to face me."

"Don't waste my time. Your days are numbered. Why draw the process out?"

"Because I know you can't win."

"I can win against a mere human any day."

Alyssa's lips slowly curved into a smile. "I think I recall a similar boast yesterday. You didn't do too well in our last encounter."

"Set the terms, human. We'll see who wins before the next day dawns."

"Come closer, Retribution. Come stand on the boundary with me."

"Step over the boundary and we'll see who wins."

Retribution moved to stand in front of her and she felt the heat pour off him. The smell of bushfires, metal and rotten eggs seared the back of her throat. She looked into his eyes, determined to win. She held up her left hand, palm out so he could see her demon mark.

"You're mine, Retribution. You claimed the name, now I invoke it. Through our tie."

"You can invoke it all you want, you have no claim over it."

Alyssa's right hand remained behind her back. She pulled out the knife she'd tucked into the waist of her jeans and grasped the blade until she felt it cut into her hand. She barely held back a hiss of pain. Blood coated the blade. She saw the flare in his eyes as he caught the scent. She loosened her grip and let the blade slip down until she held the handle.

"The battle ground's my body. Winner remains in this world." She took a step forward. One foot in sanctuary, the other out. Her right hand plunged the knife into the demon, her left arm wrapped around him. She gritted her teeth against the searing pain of his heat and the scalding blood that poured over her. She screamed out, "Retribution! I claim you. You're mine." He seemed to melt into her and the searing fire filled her body.

She dropped the knife as she fell to her knees, her head thrown back with a scream. Then she collapsed on the ground.

Chapter Twenty-Five

Alyssa opened her eyes and staggered to her feet. The heat around her made her skin feel like it'd peel away. She was in a cavern diffused with red light. Her gaze searched the area. She was alone.

"Face me, Retribution!"

"Face you! Lying, conniving, human."

Alyssa spun to find the demon towered over her. "I learned from you."

"I offered you the world. You threw it back at me. I offered to cherish you. You rejected me. All you had to do was say 'I am yours. My soul I give to you,' but you wouldn't. If you give yourself to me freely I will not make everyone your life has touched on pay in blood and scream for every second you've defied me. What is your choice, human?"

"Right now, my body will be in sanctuary. That gives me the edge. Add to that, you've given me a strong incentive to beat you. You don't understand me. You throw me down, I'll get back up. You tell me no and I'll tell you try and stop me. You threaten my friends, and I'll ask how slowly do you want to die. Don't screw with me and don't screw with my friends. You can return to hell and stay there for as long as me, or any of those my life has touched on, draws breath."

Retribution threw back his head and laughed. "Puny little human. There's no way you can make that work. You haven't the power."

"I don't." She pulled the cross from her throat and wrapped the leather around her left hand so it dangled in mid-air. "But he does." Her hand clenched into a fist and she held it in front of her at head height. "And I believe in him every bit as much as I believe in you."

"You lie!"

"Look into my eyes and tell me if I lie. I'll probably be the worst of sinners, and I'll never be able to forgive my enemies, but if I have to choose someone then it certainly won't be you. This is my body. My soul. There's no room in it for you."

"No!"

Alyssa advanced on Retribution. "Yes." She paused and thought of what Blake had told her about praying. It was worth a try. "Please God, help me. Help me send this demon back to where he belongs."

"No!" The demon burst into flames, the heat skyrocketed. He pointed at Alyssa. "You will kneel to me. You will claim your soul as mine."

"Our Father, who art in heaven, hallowed be thy name."

"You can't win. While you're stuck here, Nathan's on his way. I showed him where you were before I came for you. Your blood will stain the ground and bring me forth. You'll all die."

Alyssa hesitated. She had to warn them.

Retribution grinned, the flames dying down. "Death is so final for humans."

Alyssa took a deep breath. Until Retribution was gone none of them were safe. She tried to think of the lines that came next.

"I can feel him drawing closer. His anger is a thing of beauty. Tangible. And he's going to destroy you. I will enjoy every second of your destruction."

Never. She wouldn't let it. The words she sought filled her mind. "Thy Kingdom come, thy will be done."

The demon shrieked and flames exploded around him. "You'll die in agony. All of you. I'm going to tear each of you apart. Shred you."

Alyssa forced herself to ignore his threats and continued to pray. The flames around the demon grew higher. Until she finally said, "Amen."

The flames flared up until the demon couldn't be seen. She shielded her face from the heat, dropping her arm when they died back. There was nothing. No demon. No sign he'd ever existed. She looked around, turning, but couldn't see him. Nor could she smell the scent of him.

She grinned, triumph filling her for a second until she realised she had a problem. There was no green and white sign flashing the word exit. Panic started to rush in and she closed her eyes. She took a deep breath to calm herself before she opened her eyes. Another deep breath and she called, "Blake! I need you!" Her words echoed around the cavern. "Blake!"

She took a step forward and everything went hazy. The next thing she knew, she lay in the grass, a lantern to one side and Blake centimetres from her. She closed her eyes in relief.

"Allie Cat."

She reached up to Blake and stopped as she saw the blood on her hand and arm. She was surprised to see the thin cut still bled. Blake pressed an already bloodstained cloth into her hand.

"You're never to do that again, my Allie Cat.

When you called my name…" Blake swallowed hard, and pressed her closed hand to his cheek, leaving a red stain behind.

"I couldn't find my way out." She reached out to him with her other hand and saw the leather necklace was wrapped around it, the cross dangling. She dropped her hand.

"I was worried about that."

"Blake." She closed her eyes and tried again. The words tumbled over themselves. "I love you." She opened her eyes.

Blake smiled and gently brushed her hair back from her forehead. "I love you too, Allie Cat." He lightly kissed her. "But you're really going to have to work on this bad habit you have of scaring the hell out of me."

Alyssa smiled wryly. "I'll try, but don't hold your breath. You know what it's like. Curiosity often makes me forget to look before I leap."

"Allie." Scarlett came over to kneel beside her. "The demon? Has he gone?"

Alyssa stilled. She frowned. A smile erased it. "Yes. Yes! He's gone."

Scarlet rose to her feet. "Good."

"Oh, no." Alyssa sat up and Blake had to quickly

move out of the way. "Nathan! The demon told Nathan where to find us."

Scarlett stared at Alyssa for a moment. "Let's pack up and get out of here."

Alyssa put her necklace back on before she allowed Blake to bind her hand and clean up some of the blood on her. The rest packed and got rid of the blood on the ground. They'd barely finished when a car raced towards them out of the night. Alyssa started to head to the four-wheel-drive, but Blake clasped her shoulder so she couldn't move.

"Let's face him, Allie Cat. We need to deal with him so we can get our lives back."

Alyssa nodded and even though she wanted to run, she stood by Blake's side. She watched as Nathan climbed out of the car. He seemed to be alone, but well armed. He pointed two guns at them.

"You're wasting your time," Blake said. "The demon's been returned to the world it came from."

"Then I can shoot each of you and be done with it," Nathan said.

"Give it up, Nathan. You've lost." Blake didn't take his gaze off Nathan. He gave no indication Riley and Alex silently closed in on him.

"What I want and what I'll have is Allie for a

sacrifice. There're plenty of demons down there. And plenty of ways to make money."

"You've lost. It's done. Stop obsessing and do something useful with your life," Scarlett said.

"Useful! Is that the reason you gave yourselves to justify leaking the information of our financial situation to the press?" Nathan demanded.

"Forget about it, Nathan. It's over and done with. Put it behind you and try and make some money honestly," Scarlett said.

Alex and Riley leapt from the shadows and attacked Nathan, which sent his guns flying. Alyssa raced forward and grabbed them. She reluctantly gave them to Blake when he came to stand beside her, his hand out.

As soon as Nathan was tied to a tree, Riley said, "We all passed along the information your company was belly up."

"I'm surprised it took the vultures as long as it did to swoop in to pick through the carcass," Alex said.

Scarlett grinned. "I can see why they left his carcass alone though. Not worth the effort. Come on. Let's go home."

Riley grinned at Scarlett, "You do realise Father Joe'll have you saying penance for that comment."

Scarlet nodded. "Yes, and I really will try and feel regret for having said it."

"You can't leave me here," Nathan roared.

Alyssa stared at him. It was hard to believe that only a week had passed since she'd climbed into his car. It felt like she'd lived a lifetime. She took her cleaned knife from its sheath and strode towards Nathan. His boyish face was filled with panic. She felt no pity. She also felt no anger.

"What are you going to do, Allie? I did my best to make it easy on you. Surely you remember that."

Alyssa squatted in front of Nathan, still holding the knife. "You will leave my family alone. You will leave Erin alone."

"You can't harm me. If you use that knife on me it'll be the last thing you do."

Alyssa shook her head. "Still issuing threats? You're done. Don't you get it? And if I did use this knife on you, I wouldn't let you live."

"Allie Cat, what are you thinking?"

She ignored Blake. "You will stay out of my life." She pointed at Nathan with the knife.

"If you kill me, Brian will make sure you pay."

"And he'd fail just like you have." She stabbed the knife into the ground, well away from Nathan. "I don't need this anymore. Thanks for letting me borrow it. It was a great help in sending the demon home."

"No!"

Alyssa smiled. "Yes. Guess you should be more careful what you leave lying around."

"Bitch!"

Alyssa shook her head slowly. "I really should feel pity for you, Nathan. The day'll come when you'll have to pay for your sins and I wouldn't be in your shoes for the whole world. Not even if it came gift wrapped and was placed in my palm." She rose to her feet, walked away from him and ignored the abuse he yelled at her.

Blake dropped his arm around her shoulders as she reached his side. "You had me worried for a minute there."

Alyssa laughed. "I wasn't even tempted."

"You ready to go home, Allie Cat?"

"Yes."

Nathan screamed, "I'm going to make sure every single one of you pays."

Alex took a couple of steps towards Nathan. "I've already rung someone to come and collect you. And I know we don't have enough proof to press charges. That it would only be our word against yours, but our family will keep you under surveillance.

Everything you do, everywhere you go, someone'll be watching you. And when you slip up, we'll use that proof to make sure you serve time."

Nathan glared at them. The light from the lantern Alex carried sent shadows dancing across his wary face, but he fell silent. Even when they turned, walked away and climbed in their vehicle, he stayed quiet.

"Is it safe to leave him here? What if he escapes?" Alyssa asked. The lantern sat on the floor in the back of the vehicle, casting shadowy light on them.

Riley shook his head. "I'm not that bad at tying knots. Don't worry, someone'll be here within a couple of hours to get him. He's not going anywhere."

"That's good. And I'd rather not stick around that long." As Alex started the four-wheel-drive she leaned against Blake, who had his arms around her. Her gaze went to Scarlett in the front passenger seat. "I heard what you said to Nathan. I bet it felt good."

"Stop corrupting my cousin," Blake murmured against the top of her head.

Alyssa turned to Blake. "Now what?"

"Now we take you home to your parents," Blake said. "Although we probably should clean you up first. The blood might upset them."

Alyssa closed her eyes before she spoke. "Don't toy with me, Blake." Her eyes opened when she felt his hand cup her face.

"I'm sorry. But that isn't negotiable. You will return home and," he pressed his fingers against her lips when she would've spoken. "And you will go to uni next year like you planned. If your parents ground you, we'll work around that. But I'm thinking even they'd at least let me take you to church on Sunday."

Alyssa grinned and threw her arms around Blake. "That better not be the only place you're planning on taking me. If they ever let me out of the house for anything other than uni."

For answer, Blake's lips lightly brushed across Alyssa's.

"I hate to interrupt such a touching scene." Riley grinned at them.

"I'm sure, you do, Ry," Blake said dryly.

"Does this mean you're back in the family business?"

Blake looked at his arm. His mark now travelled several centimetres beyond the crimson tattoo barbs. His gaze went to Alyssa's hair and the crimson lock that streaked through it. "What do you say, Allie Cat?"

"Me?"

"Yeah. How do you feel about me putting myself between demons and the rest of the world?"

"Well, I guess it'd be okay if I was standing there beside you."

Blake turned to his brother. "There's your answer, Ry."

Riley held out his left hand and Blake clasped his hand to his brother's forearm so their wrists touched. He grinned. "Welcome back, brother."

Free Ebook

Subscribe to Avril's newsletter to receive a free ebook. This ebook is exclusive to those on her mailing list. To find out more about this offer visit: www.avrilsabine.com/free-ebook.

*

We value your privacy and will not sell, rent, exchange or loan your email address to third parties. Your information is confidential and you are under no obligation to remain on the mailing list and can unsubscribe at any time.

Acknowledgements

Thank you to all those who put in long hours helping me improve this story and pointing out the areas that needed work. You know who you are, I'm sure you don't need me to tell you.

To The Reader

If you enjoyed this book, why not consider leaving a review to help other readers discover it too? Reader engagement is one of the few ways that lets an author know readers want more books in a particular series or genre. So leave a review and tell friends, not only about this book but also about other ones you've enjoyed, so you can continue to enjoy books by your favourite authors for years to come.

Dreams are meant to be lived,

Avril

About The Author

Avril is an Australian author who lives with her family on acreage in South East Queensland. She writes mostly young adult speculative fiction, but has been known to dabble in other genres. You can find more information about her at her website www.avrilsabine.com where you can also subscribe to her newsletter to be kept informed about new releases, current projects, blog posts and exclusive news.

Titles By Avril Sabine

Stories about strong characters and characters who discover their strengths.

SERIES

Assassins Of The Dead- Young Adult Fantasy/ Paranormal

Book 1: Dark Blade

Book 2: Dragon Touched

Book 3: Society Against Vampires

Book 4: King's Request

Book 5: Duke's Courier

Book 6: Necromancer Resistance

Dragon Blood- Young Adult Urban Fantasy Romance (5 book series)

Book 1: Pliethin

Book 2: Wyvern

Book 3: Surety

Book 4: Knight

Book 5: Mage

Dragon Mage- Young Adult Urban Fantasy Romance (Series two of Dragon Blood series)

Book 1: Promise

Book 2: Betrayed

Dragon Blood Chronicles- Young Adult Urban Fantasy Romance

(Companion stand alone series to Dragon Blood)

Book 1: Oath

Book 2: Betrayed

Guardians Of The Round Table- Young Adult Fantasy LitRPG

(Co-written with Storm and Rhys Petersen)

Book 1: Dexterity Fail

Book 2: Goblin Boots

Book 3: Singed Feathers

Book 4: Frog Mage

Book 5: Crystal Mine

Book 6: Cursed Harp

Book 7: Treasure Seeker

Book 8: Bard's Hollow

Maps and lore books for the series can be found at:

www.avrilsabine.com/series/gotrt

Rosie's Rangers- Young Adult Western Steampunk

(6 book series)

Book 1: Justice

Book 2: Vengeance

Book 3: Treachery

Book 4: Accused

Book 5: Wanted

Book 6: Corruption

Mark Of Kings- Children's Fantasy

(Upper middle grade/preteen)

(4 book series)

Book 1: The Arena

Book 2: The Island

Book 3: The Assassin

Book 4: The King

Demon Hunters- Young Adult Urban Fantasy/ Horror/Romance

Book 1: Blood Sacrifice

Book 2: Retribution

Book 3: Tainted

Book 4: Premonition

Book 5: Cursed

Book 6: Feud

Book 7: Extrication

Plea Of The Damned- Young Adult Urban Fantasy/Paranormal

(6 book series)

Book 1: Forgive Me Lucy

Book 2: Forgive Me Aiden

Book 3: Forgive Me Jena

Book 4: Forgive Me Kobe

Book 5: Forgive Me Marti

Book 6: Forgive Me Dawson

Realms Of The Fae- Young Adult Urban Fantasy Romance

The Sword (short story in Like A Girl Anthology)

Heart Of Stone

Book 1: A Debt Owed

Book 2: Marked By The Hunt

Book 3: The Magic Collector

Book 4: An Unexpected Betrayal

Book 5: Imprisoned By Iron

Fairytales Retold (Short Stories)

Snow-White And Rose-Red

The Twelve Brothers

The Light Princess

Beauty And The Beast

Sleeping Beauty

Aschenputtel

The Golden Bird

The Frog Prince

The Death Of Koshchei The Deathless

Myths And Legends Retold (Short Stories)

Ion, Son Of Apollo

Sir Gawain And The Maid With The Narrow Sleeves

Princess Ilse, The Giant's Daughter

YOUNG ADULT NOVELS

Young Adult Fantasy Romance

Elf Sight

Earth Bound

Young Adult Urban Fantasy

Stone Warrior (with elements of romance)

The Jungle Inside

Young Adult Contemporary Romance

Through Your Eyes

The Ugly Stepsister

Perfect Little Princess

Young Adult Contemporary/Paranormal/Romance

Whispers In The Dark

Over Too Soon

Young Adult Sci-Fi

Experiment X-One-Six (Urban Sci-Fi/Superheroes)

An Endless Dawn (Post Apocalyptic Sci-Fi)

CHILDREN'S BOOKS

Dragon Lord (Preteen/early teens) (Fantasy)

The Irish Wizard (Upper middle grade) (Urban Fantasy)

SHORT STORIES

Urban Fantasy

Eternally Late

Dealings With Joe

Glimpses (short story in That Moment When Anthology)

Contemporary

The Brat Next Door

Fantasy LitRPG

(Set in the same world as Guardians Of The Round Table Series)

Tales Of Inadon 1: The Disc (Co-written with Storm and Rhys Petersen) (short story in Game On! Anthology)

Post Apocalyptic Sci-Fi

Compulsive Directive

NONFICTION

A Year Of Weekly Writing Exercises (Creative Writing)

Cooking For Families With Allergies (Cooking) (Co-written with Storm Petersen)

Tell Me A Story, Grandma (Memoir)

Overview Of Independently Publishing A Book (How To)

For the most up to date details on available titles visit:

www.avrilsabine.com/books/bibliography

Demon Hunter Series

To learn more about this series visit:

www.avrilsabine.com/series/dh

BOOKS AVAILABLE IN THE SERIES

Book 1: Blood Sacrifice

Book 2: Retribution

Book 3: Tainted

Book 4: Premonition

Book 5: Cursed

Book 6: Feud

Book 7: Extrication

Disclaimer

This is a work of fiction. Names, characters, businesses, places, events and incidents are either the products of the author's imagination or used in a fictitious manner. Any resemblance to actual persons, living or dead, or actual events is purely coincidental.